Penelope Grace and the Winter Carousel

Book One of

The Chronicles of Wonder

Alexandria Kyra Frederick

Penelope Grace and the Winter Carousel

Copyright © 2025 Alexandria Kyra Frederick

Cover Design by Erica Richardson

This is a work of fiction. All of the characters, places, and events portrayed in this novel are either products of the author's imagination or are used fictitiously. All characters are fictional, and any similarity to people living or dead is purely coincidental.

All rights reserved. No portion of this book may be reproduced, stored in a retrieval system, or transmitted in any form or by any means – electronic, mechanical, photocopy, recording, scanning, or other – except for brief quotations in critical reviews or articles, without prior written permission of the publisher.

From the Library of 21:25 Books

www.2125Books.com

ISBN: 978-1-7374951-3-0
Library of Congress Control Number: 2025904286
Printed in the United States of America

DEDICATION

To my mom: strong, courageous, and full of wonder.

CONTENTS

Prologue 1

Part One: Christmas 3

Part Two: Winter 29

Part Three: Apricity..80

Author's gratitude 120

PROLOGUE

Penelope Grace was a remarkable girl.

Of course, that word — remarkable — can mean many different things, depending on whom you ask.

Upon entering the Saris household, you would first be taken to the kitchen for a warm cup of tea to fight off the early winter's chill. There, Nurse Sasha — who oversaw *everything* — would happily offer you her opinion. She could hardly find it less than remarkable that a girl of sixteen could behave so like her nine-year-old brother as to be nearly indistinguishable.

Once welcomed and enlightened, you might continue to the living room and find a comfortable chair near Penelope's mother, Mary, who is patiently mending the latest torn and dirt-stained dress. She would share with you how her daughter is remarkably and admirably unconcerned with what others think of her.

Over the years, her friends marveled to find that Penelope was just as likely to pick up an imaginary sword as an intricate piece of embroidery. Growing serious now, Mary would tell you of the many encouragements she has received to rein her daughter in.

But it is too rare a gift to see a child's spirit endure into adulthood. As Penelope's mother, she would ask, how could she do less than safeguard it?

But just then, young George would come bursting in, his great-uncle Alex not far behind, and insist on knowing what your conversation was about.

"Well, George," Mary would ask with the warmest of smiles, "what do *you* think makes your sister remarkable?"

He would think hard about it for a minute or two but, his nose crinkling up as he grinned, would soon reply with a firm, "Two things."

And then, leaning forward as if to share with you a very great secret, George would tell you a story. Just last week, Penelope had, remarkably, succeeded both in assembling an entire regiment of nutcracker soldiers in the foyer and in vanishing from sight before Nurse Sasha could certainly accuse her of having done it.

"And the second?" you would ask, sincerely eager to know.

"She is the only grown-up who isn't only teasing me when she says she still believes in Father Christmas."

Equally impressed by both these reasons, you might then turn to great-uncle Alex, whom you would find no less willing to join in the conversation.

He would have to say that Penelope was remarkable for her persistent delight in all things simple, yet extraordinary. Even now she remains as enchanted with his magic tricks as she was on the day he first arrived from Greece to share them with her.

But of all her family, acquaintances, and friends, only her father, John – who has been listening by the crackling fire all the while – could tell you with absolute certainty what it was that made Penelope Grace genuinely remarkable:

"Wonder."

PART ONE: CHRISTMAS

Often, you will find that people long for the warmer months of the year. Perhaps, you rejoice in the brilliant blooms of spring and the feeling of the warm sun on your skin. While she would certainly not argue against the beauty of those things, Penelope Grace delighted most in winter.

Where some saw harshness and gloom, she saw the thrill of expectation. As the first snow fell, Penelope would rush her family out of doors, exhilarated as she breathed in the stillness God ushered in with the first flakes. She would stand in the middle of their quiet street, face tilted up and eyes closed, listening as He whispered to her about the wonder of what was coming.

Hope built in her heart throughout the whole of winter; while many could only see the death of things above, Penelope Grace remembered what was happening out of sight, beneath the frozen ground. The flowers and trees were only preparing to grow again, waiting to burst into new life, and Penelope Grace waited with them. With so much expectation, it is no surprise that as Christmas drew near, Penelope celebrated with more joy than you would believe one human heart capable of holding.

Her spirit was contagious, and none left her company without firmly believing that winter was the most wonderful of seasons and Christmas the holiday to be cherished most.

But what of you, reader?

Well, let us see if she can convince you.

The candles were among the first of the Christmas decorations to arrive and these, above all, were her favorite. Each year, on the same day in early November, Penelope Grace lovingly placed each one upon the windowsills and the cherry wood mantelpiece.

Follow me, and that is where we will find her this evening.

George trailed behind her as she moved to the nearest street-facing window, candle in hand. Setting it down, Penelope turned to her brother, a smile lighting up her hazel eyes.

"Here, Georgie, you light this one."

Beaming with pride that he should be chosen for such a task, he gingerly took the match from Penelope's hand. Carefully now, he lit the candle, watching with delight as its small, but brilliant, light bathed the windowsill in a comforting warm glow.

"Why the candles first, Penelope?" George asked, his voice soft.

She looked out at their quiet, cobblestone street for a moment before answering. "Because, Georgie, they remind us of what we're really celebrating. Light coming into the world."

He smiled, staying with her a moment more before running to join Uncle Alex by the fire.

Penelope Grace turned to look at her family. Georgie sat in Uncle Alex's lap, learning to play cards, and her mother and father laughed softly together nearby. She cherished the moment, marveling at the way their home had been transformed by nothing more than a few candles, by warmth and light.

It was several weeks later – the 13th of December to be precise – when the evening of the Gardener's annual Christmas party arrived. Though

Penelope loved holiday parties, the Gardener's was an altogether stuffy affair, and she searched for reasons not to attend with great enthusiasm.

The atmosphere was stifling; every decoration was in its proper place, and Penelope always suspected that Mr. and Mrs. Gardener had sacrificed joy for the sake of perfection. She enjoyed attending until, at the age of fourteen, she made the alarming discovery that all her playmates were so determined to grow up that they had forgotten how to have fun.

Last year, she had claimed to be much too tired from December's merriment to accompany her parents. But this year, her father knew just what she was up to. Dressed in his most excellent suit, he looked down at her, trying to look stern, and failing miserably.

"Now, Penelope," he asked with a knowing smile, "what excuse will I give for you this year? The Gardeners will be devastated by your absence. They so enjoyed the mock sword fight you incited amongst the children three Christmases ago."

Penelope laughed, remembering how she and her friend, Charlie, had been shocked to discover that their Christmas crackers were actually swords. Even more horrifying, the Gardener's dog was a terrifying beast threatening the well-being of the guests. It had been quick work to convince all the children that they must defend the Gardener's home. Soon enough, they were charging through the house, to the confusion of everyone present, and the extreme alarm of the Gardener's unlucky Spaniel.

"Do they still talk about that?" she asked in mock innocence.

"With great fear of reprisal," her father replied, a mischievous gleam in his eyes.

Still laughing, Penelope said, "Oh Papa, I would much rather keep Uncle Alex and Georgie company."

He bent down to kiss her softly on the top of her head. "Then, my dearest Penelope Grace, you are hereby released from all obligation to attend the Gardener's Christmas party. And I must admit," he continued quietly, "I am in full agreement that your Uncle Alex's company will be far more fun."

Just then, Penelope felt a soft tug on her hand. She looked down to find Georgie standing beside her, his brown eyes full of hope. "Penelope, will you be staying home with me?"

She smiled, ruffling his hair fondly as she knelt before him. "Of course I'm staying, Georgie. Where else could I have such fun?"

He beamed up at her, his joy spilling over, and then ran down the hall, shouting on his way, "I'll tell Uncle Alex! He'll do his magic tricks for us!"

Her father let out a hearty laugh as he and Penelope watched young George slip and slide across the freshly polished floor, in his eagerness to share the news. Mary paused just in time to prevent a collision with her youngest as he charged by before continuing on her way, graceful as ever in her dark green evening gown.

Penelope admired the gown's beautifully embroidered flowers and the small beads that glittered as they caught the candlelight. Her mother looked radiant.

"Do look after your brother and uncle, Penelope," Mary said, not at all surprised that her daughter was not accompanying them. "Oh, and try not to run Nurse Sasha out of the house," she continued, a small smile causing her dimples to show.

"You underestimate Nurse Sasha, my dear," John chided. "I expect she'll manage." Turning to Penelope, he said, "I also expect to hear reports of an altogether adventurous evening when we return."

Laughing, she replied, "We'll do our best, Papa," before following them out onto the front step. She smiled at the familiar sound of her father whistling his favorite tune as he helped her mother into the carriage. Long after they had pulled away, Penelope lingered outside, delighting in the touch of the freshly fallen, powdery snow against her bare feet.

Their already quiet street was transformed by the shimmering snowflakes, for snow brings a stillness that you cannot encounter at any other time of year. Penelope could not help but enjoy the sensation for a few breaths.

Soon enough, she heard the creak of their door behind her. "Penelope?" Uncle Alex inquired, his voice rich and warm. Seeing her standing in the cold, he smiled, unsurprised.

"Ah, yes. My winter princess." Uncle Alex looked up to the sky, admiring the winter night for himself. "Well, follow me, Princess Penelope," he continued, bowing formally. "The young prince is becoming impatient for dinner."

They re-entered just as George was running toward the entryway, Nurse Sasha close behind.

He stopped just shy of stepping on Penelope's toes. "We should eat," he pronounced with great exuberance.

"We should, Georgie, but first we have a crucial decision to make. Papa has told me that we must have an adventurous evening. Do you have any ideas?"

Instantly, he grinned, and Penelope knew he had thought of just the thing. "Share them with me?"

George beckoned Penelope to come close before whispering in her ear. Agreeing that it was a brilliant plan, she, in turn, shared it with Uncle Alex in hushed tones. The lines around his eyes crinkled as he smiled; even at seventy-six, he had lost none of his delight for all things mischievous and playful.

"Dare I ask what devastating consequences await those who fail to carry out this mission?" Uncle Alex questioned.

Another mischievous grin from George. "They must surrender their share of dessert to me."

"A just punishment," Uncle Alex replied. With a very grave expression, he bowed to his nephew, and George, fighting a smile, returned the gesture before scampering off to decide how he might best contribute to the mischief.

Nurse Sasha, flabbergasted by the lot of them, shuddered to think what shenanigans she might soon be exposed to and retreated to the kitchen.

Penelope Grace braced herself before entering the dining area, knowing that the moment she did, all sorts of silliness would ensue. George had told Uncle Alex and herself that they must find the most ridiculous costumes imaginable. But he gave them this warning: once they all sat down for supper, they must not, under any circumstances, laugh.

It can only seem fair that Penelope Grace set out to create a costume so absurd that George could not hope to win at his own mischievous game.

Taking a deep breath, she entered the room to find their plates already filled with piping hot food and Uncle Alex sitting in great state at the head of the table.

A soft purple blanket was wrapped around his shoulders, secured by what Penelope suspected was one of Mama's favorite brooches. But by far the most amusing was the Christmas wreath, full of pine cones and bright red ribbon, sitting on top of his head – a makeshift crown, she guessed.

He gestured for her to sit down. It was then that she noticed the umbrella. He planted it firmly on the carpet, as if it were some sort of grand staff, and met Penelope's gaze, daring her not to be amused. The laughter nearly escaped her then.

Adopting a solemn expression, she adjusted her makeshift sword belt – made out of evergreen garland and very uncomfortable indeed – before striding forward with the utmost confidence. Regretfully, she only managed a few steps before she tripped over her weapon of choice: Nurse Sasha's broom. Penelope looked up quickly, though, hoping to catch Uncle Alex in a laugh, but was chagrined to find that he was maintaining his composure.

He cleared his throat as she took a seat with as much dignity as possible. "A most unfortunate choice for a sword," he lamented, before quickly taking a drink. But Penelope smiled, knowing he was really trying to disguise a laugh.

"Where is Georgie?" she asked. No sooner had the words left her lips then she heard her brother clearing his throat just outside the door.

"Tonight, Penelope," he declared in a very dignified tone, "I am Sir George, a noble knight, and defender of the realm!"

He entered the room then, and Penelope knew she could not hope to find a more striking figure in all England. She first noticed one of Nurse Sasha's freshly ironed tablecloths draped dramatically across Sir George's shoulders and secured with a clothespin.

In his right hand, he held a whisk, a weapon sure to inspire fear in the hearts of the land's greatest enemies. Slowly, he approached the table. Penelope and Uncle Alex could only assume this was to give them more time to admire his nobility. Once seated, Sir George observed them both carefully for any sign of merriment.

So far, they had contained it, but Penelope could not resist the urge to tease her brother. George, however, beat her to it. "How are you enjoying Sherwood Forest, Penelope?"

She hesitated, confused, before remembering that her hat for this evening was borrowed from their many games of Robin Hood. "Oh, it's lovely this time of year," she replied, "though the Sheriff is giving us untold trouble, as always. I do hope you can find time in between quests to visit us."

"I would like that very much."

They sat in silence for a few minutes, each devising the best way to make the others laugh. Eventually, Penelope landed on just the thing. "Sir George, I hesitate to mention this, but I cannot help but notice that your helmet has several holes in it."

He adjusted the colander indignantly. "It is the consequence of my many daring escapades."

"Of course," Penelope replied with a small smile. "Forgive me."

At this point, Uncle Alex interjected, "Sir George, I wonder if you would be so kind as to share some tales of these daring escapades with us."

"Yes, it would be my honor."

His tone was very formal and impressive, but Penelope had to confess that the effect was somewhat spoiled when the colander slipped down over his eyes.

Her laughter nearly bubbled over, and Penelope looked down quickly, pursing her lips and fighting to mask it.

George, instantly noticing her difficulty with immense delight, asked with the sincerest of looks, "Is there something sour on your plate, my lady?"

Penelope cleared her throat before answering. "On the contrary, Sir George, the food is, as always, delicious."

"I'm so happy to hear that," he replied with a grin, fully intending to tease her further.

But just at that moment, Nurse Sasha came bustling in. She glanced at them briefly as she placed dessert on the table, then gave a start and looked back. They met her startled expression with perfect innocence, as if nothing at all was out of the ordinary, save George, who refused to make eye contact.

After a flabbergasted silence, Nurse Sasha seemed about to leave well enough alone until she took a good look at George's costume. "George," she managed to sputter, "is that my tablecloth?"

"No," he said with admirable restraint, before quickly looking away for something more interesting to stare at.

Nurse Sasha crossed her arms and began to tap her foot, fully aware of his ploy. "George," she said expectantly.

He turned back to face her with a startled look, as if only just realizing that she was there. "Yes?"

"My whisk, if you please."

Slowly, and with great dignity, he passed the whisk to Nurse Sasha, who promptly snatched it from his hand and exited the room with much huffing and muttering.

Uncle Alex, Penelope, and George sat quietly for perhaps three seconds before they burst out laughing, unable to restrain their joy any longer.

"I believe this calls for chocolate cake by the fire," Uncle Alex said. The joyous delight in his eyes would have convinced even the strictest of parents that it was an excellent idea. It was certainly enough to persuade George, who rushed to get three plates.

Penelope smiled. "I'll be there shortly, Uncle Alex. Save me a piece?"

"Of course."

Penelope gathered their dinner plates and carried them to the kitchen. Between their many mischievous exploits and the care of the household itself, Nurse Sasha did quite enough for them already and would, perhaps, appreciate some help. She had just finished washing the dishes when Nurse Sasha arrived, carrying what remained of her chocolate cake.

When she saw what Penelope had done, she said, "Oh, just when I was fixing to stay angry with you for that mountain of nutcracker soldiers!"

"What soldiers?" Penelope asked before dancing from the room, the faintest hint of a smile in her eyes.

She found Uncle Alex and Georgie wrapped in blankets near the fire, their empty plates next to them. Finding her own blanket and cake, Penelope settled in beside them to listen to the last of Uncle Alex's story. It was a familiar tale, but she, like George, never tired of hearing it. Both leaned forward with delight as Uncle Alex's story came alive. It was as if the very scene he described was taking place in the room. Treacherous waves rose above the furniture, threatening to sweep them away along with a much younger Uncle Alex, who had just braved the dangers of the sea to save their grandpa, George.

They gasped as Uncle Alex dove into its depths, heedless of all danger to himself so long as his brother was safe. Still, none could deny the shiver that ran through them as an impossibly large tentacle glided past Uncle Alex in the dark water. He peered all around, trying to discern where the beast had gone, but he could find no sign of it.

Uncertain, he swam forward several feet, and suddenly, it was too late to turn back. Two tentacles shot out of the darkness, binding his legs together as what felt like hundreds of sharp-toothed suckers pierced his skin. With his arms still free, Uncle Alex managed to remove his knife from its sheath, intent on breaking the beast's hold until he caught sight of his brother wrapped in its tentacles and inching closer to its gruesome beak.

Praying he could stay conscious long enough to free them both, Uncle Alex waited as he was drawn into an unforgiving cage of tentacles. He gripped his knife, preparing to strike at the limb wrapped around his brother's middle as soon as he was within reach. He counted the tortuous heartbeats until the moment came, and plunged the blade into the beast.

Surprised by the sudden assault, the brothers' attacker loosened its grip on George, giving Uncle Alex the opportunity he needed to draw George out of the mass of tentacles as he continued slashing at the monstrous creature.

Relief flooded him as he saw the last of the bloodied tentacles slip away from his brother, but all relief was quickly swallowed up by fear as Uncle Alex felt the limbs around his own body grip him with renewed force, wrenching him away from George, who now began to descend into the water's depths.

A fierce determination seized Uncle Alex; after all they had been through, he would not lose his brother now. He struck out at the beast desperately, despite knowing that the real battle was no longer with this creature of the sea, but with his own ability to stay conscious.

After suffering several sharp jabs into its tentacles, the beast, finally cowed by the repeated attacks, released Uncle Alex and retreated into the darkness of the ocean's deepest waters. Fighting the unrelenting blurriness of his vision, Uncle Alex dove down, fighting to reach his brother in time. A few desperate moments passed, and Uncle Alex felt George's hand in his own. He struggled to reach the surface, but his strength finally left him, and they both began to sink.

Georgie cried out, despairing that Uncle Alex would ever reach the surface, but Penelope remembered well what was coming next, and it filled her with a fiery hope.

"The waters were sure to claim us," Uncle Alex said in whispered tones, "and yet, when next I opened my eyes, my brother and I lay on the deck, unnoticed amidst our comrades' attempts to battle the storm."

His voice faded, the treacherous waters and the dangers they held slowly receded from the room, and all were safe and warm by the fireplace once again.

"But *who* saved you?" George cried.

"It remains a mystery, I suppose," Uncle Alex replied, though Penelope knew by the smile on his face that he didn't really believe it was a mystery at all. "All I can say for certain, George, is that when, by all accounts, we should have been sinking, we were lifted up out of the water." They passed a few moments in silence, each staring into the fire.

"Uncle Alex, will you do your magic trick now?" George asked, his request punctuated by an enormous yawn.

"Of course. Anything for Sir George."

Uncle Alex rose to place another chair close beside his own. George sat up in anticipation, wide awake once more.

Uncle Alex returned to his chair and then promptly ignored the two of them as he stared into the fire again. And so it was that, without any sign of Uncle Alex having done a thing, the chair beside him began to float.

George shot up to run around the chairs, but even with the closest of inspections, there was no evidence to suggest that Uncle Alex had any hand in the chair's sudden levitation. George – foiled once again – returned to his seat, and the chair to the floor.

But after only a few seconds, he could no longer contain himself. "How do you do it? Please tell me, Uncle Alex, *please?*"

"No, Georgie," Penelope said, laughing. "We mustn't learn his secret."

"But why?" he replied, thoroughly disgruntled.

"Because it's more enchanting this way." She rose and held out her hand to him. "Now, come and get ready for bed, and I'll tell you a story about St. George that no one else has ever heard before."

George took her hand, but with a very skeptical expression on his face. "What do people *not* know about St. George?"

"Well, that he was not a dragon slayer as many believe, but a great champion of the winged creatures, determined to see every last one to safety."

"What will his story be like?" George asked as they began to climb the stairs.

"He will have to embark on a quest and brave calamitous seas and unknown lands if he ever hopes to find the perfect home for them."

"Will it be dangerous?"

"Oh yes," Penelope answered, "but worth it to see them safe."

Uncle Alex looked after them fondly as they made their way upstairs. Once again, his eyes returned to the fire, and he sat there quietly for several minutes before taking a small jewelry box from his pocket and holding it carefully in his hand.

He believed that time was slipping from him, yet he could not help but feel that tonight was not the right moment to give the locket to her, though he had promised her grandmother, Mary, that he would do so.

Uncle Alex hesitated a moment more but returned the box to his pocket just as Penelope took her seat by the fire. He was not quick enough, though, to keep her from noticing the sudden quiet of his mood.

"Are you all right, Uncle Alex?" Penelope asked.

He looked at her for a long moment before speaking, hoping that she felt how loved she was and how proud he was of her. Gathering the right words, he said quietly, "One day, my dear girl, you may be told to grow up, to think yourself wise and clever. Everything worthwhile is lost this way. You were created to weave joy and delight – wonder – into people's lives again, and it is when you are at your most child-like that you do this best."

"Why are you saying this, Uncle Alex?" she asked, finding herself near tears and not quite knowing why.

"Because I want you to remember, my sweetest Penelope Grace. I want you to remember."

She could think of nothing to say. She could only feel that of all the words Uncle Alex had spoken to her, these were the most worthy of remembering.

Penelope jumped as the front door opened, and her parents' voices filled the hall. Her father entered the room, all warmth and laughter, followed closely by her mother.

"And was an adventurous evening had by all?" her father asked, a broad grin lighting up his face.

"Yes, Papa," Penelope answered, managing a small smile.

Her father frowned as he knelt beside her. "And a good one, I hope?"

"Yes, I'm just tired, Papa."

"Hmmm. Off to bed then."

"I will in a moment. I'd like to enjoy the fire."

"All right," he replied, though he wondered at her quiet mood.

Tender hugs and kisses and wishes for sweet dreams were exchanged by all. Penelope's parents went upstairs, and it was not long before Uncle Alex followed. Penelope remained where she was, watching Uncle Alex make his slow way up the steps, surprising herself by wondering for the first time how many more evenings like this one she had left to share with him.

He faded quickly after that night.

For several days, Uncle Alex managed to keep it to himself, easy enough to do when everyone was swept up in Christmas festivities. He failed, however, to account for Nurse Sasha's attentive eye. She was the first to notice that he was only picking at his food. Initially believing that there must be something in her cooking that was troubling his stomach, she searched for recipes that would agree with him.

Nothing she tried worked. After a week passed, Nurse Sasha decided that she had held her tongue quite long enough, and she took her suspicions to Penelope's father. That evening, Penelope and George listened just outside the door as their parents questioned Uncle Alex.

"Uncle, why did you not say something?" Papa asked. "We must call the doctor."

"No, John. I will not spend Christmas in a hospital."

"But surely," Mama said, "if you are unwell, and they can help, it will be worth it."

But Uncle Alex shook his head, sure of his decision and more stubborn than all of them combined. "The moment the festivities are over, I promise you, you may call the doctor without argument from me. Until then, we will enjoy our time together."

Recognizing when a battle was lost, Mama and Papa conceded. Penelope and George rushed away to avoid being caught eavesdropping. George seemed encouraged by the news that Uncle Alex would be home for Christmas, but Penelope, once alone in the quiet of her room, felt apprehension swell within her.

Yet, when the next day came, all her misgivings seemed to be for nothing. Uncle Alex, feeling better than ever, joined them for breakfast, and their Christmas preparations continued without any shadow of fear to darken them. It wasn't until the following evening after a group of good friends had left that all their concerns returned, and they could not keep them at bay this time, no matter how they tried.

They had just finished a game of cards when Uncle Alex sat forward in his chair suddenly as if trying to fight off a sharp pain.

"Instantly, John was beside him. "Uncle?"

"I'm fine, John," Uncle Alex insisted, though none believed him. "I'd like to lie down, that's all. Penelope, dear, I wonder if you might help me with the stairs?"

"Of course," she replied, rising quickly as Papa helped him up from the chair.

As they took a few slow steps together, John whispered to Penelope, "Can you manage?"

"Yes," she answered, confident that, for Uncle Alex, she could.

They were only a quarter of the way up the stairs when he fell.

"Papa," she cried, and he was there, lifting Uncle Alex in his arms.

He started up the steps, but Uncle Alex, speaking impossibly softly, said, "No. I want to be near you all."

Without questioning him, John returned to the family room, taking great care as he laid Uncle Alex down gently on the sofa. As soon as he had made Uncle Alex comfortable, he shot into action. "Penelope, George, we need something more comfortable for him to wear. Mary, some blankets and pillows?"

"Of course, dear," she said with all tenderness before hurrying up the steps, Penelope and George close behind her.

Having heard the commotion, Nurse Sasha bustled in. "Sir?"

John tuned, his expression more grave than she had ever seen in all her time with the family. "Fetch the doctor."

Within a few minutes, they all returned, save Nurse Sasha, anxious to see all of Uncle Alex's needs met, to find some way to make him well. But eventually, their ideas ran short, and they each surrendered at last to sitting and waiting and listening to the ticking clock grow louder.

They all jumped when the front door opened, signaling Nurse Sasha's return. When she entered the room and met all their expectant gazes, she looked like someone who has news they do not want to share.

"There's been an emergency elsewhere. The doctor cannot come until tomorrow."

No one said anything, but Penelope, sitting close beside her father, could feel the dread creeping over him. She took his hand, hoping to fight against it when he, perhaps, could not. Everyone vowed to pass the night by Uncle Alex's side. Papa tried to protest, arguing that everyone else ought to get a decent night's rest, but they were all of them determined, and blankets and pillows were brought down and arranged.

No one could sleep.

While the rest of the family settled down in their makeshift beds, Penelope's father alternated between keeping an anxious watch at Uncle Alex's side and pacing with increasing agitation about the room.

It was during one of his renewed attempts at pacing that George snuggled close and asked Penelope to tell him a story. She quickly obliged, happy for the comfort of a good story like one Uncle Alex might tell. She had only just begun to weave the tale when their father abruptly stopped in front of them.

"No. No stories tonight, children."

George began to cry, not understanding their father's unusually harsh tone. Penelope held him close. "Shh, it will be all right, Georgie," she said. "Just hold my hand until you fall asleep."

Very little time passed before she felt her little brother's breathing deepen, and she prayed he was at least finding some comfort while he dreamed. Nurse Sasha was the next to give in to exhaustion, while Papa remained just as ill at ease as before.

Mary left him to his own devices for quite some time before finally rising. In hushed tones, she tried to calm him. "John, you do him no good by being so restless. You must rest. He will need you in the morning."

John wrestled for a moment with the desire to argue with her wisdom, but he bowed his head, his shoulders beginning to shake as Mary held him. With great tenderness and boundless patience, Mary helped him arrange some blankets on the floor next to the sofa where Uncle Alex fitfully slept. Once done, they both settled down to sleep at last.

Penelope breathed a sigh of relief, longing for sleep herself. Yet, no matter how many slow, deep breaths she took, anything resembling rest eluded her for some time. She kept returning to her father's words. *No, no stories tonight.* She feared that he might have forgotten what he had spent all their lives teaching them: that it was on nights like this one that stories were needed most.

Sometime later, in the middle of the night, Penelope Grace woke with a start. She propped herself up to look about the room. Everyone else seemed to be sleeping peacefully, save for her father, who sat with his head lying on Uncle Alex's shoulder.

Penelope frowned, for when she looked at her father, he seemed faint, as if something was blocking her view of him. She rubbed her eyes and peered closer, only to find that the blurriness was gone. Dismissing it as a trick of the low firelight or of her own exhaustion, Penelope went to sit beside her father, wrapping her blanket around him as she did so. They looked at each other for a long moment – her hazel eyes a perfect reflection of his own – saying nothing, and knowing they did not need to.

Light filtered through the curtains, but Penelope Grace found that her father's mood had only darkened with the coming of morning. She looked at Uncle Alex and understood why.

He looked terribly pale, and his breathing was shallow. Usually so full of strength and bold joy, Uncle Alex would never have been described as a frail man, and Penelope's heart ached to see him looking so small. Her father still knelt beside him. He looked shaken, stunned that he really could lose the one he treasured as a father. Penelope reached out for his hand, longing to comfort him, but he seemed not to notice her.

Penelope started as Mama gently took her by the shoulders and led her to the kitchen, where George sat with Nurse Sasha, picking at his breakfast.

Penelope turned to look up at her mother. "Mama, I don't want to leave."

"I will stay with your father, dear," Mary reassured, placing a cool hand on Penelope's cheek. "Right now, your brother needs you."

Knowing Mama was right, she took her seat next to Georgie and offered him a small smile, which he was thoroughly unimpressed by. Nevertheless, Penelope Grace was undeterred. It only took a moment for the perfect idea to occur to her, and much to Nurse Sasha's frustration, Penelope left the room. When she returned, she handed a blanket to George, who had looked chilled, wrapped another round her own shoulders, and began to devour her breakfast.

George stared at her, incredulous. "What are you doing?" he asked.

She gave him a look, as though it should have been obvious. "There was a Wilderbeast at our door in the night. We need to keep up our strength."

"There's no such thing as a Wilderbeast," he retorted with an unamused frown.

Penelope Grace shrugged her shoulder. "If you don't believe me, go to the door and see for yourself."

He immediately ran off, determined to prove her wrong. Though it was hard to play and imagine, Penelope was comforted by knowing that this was just what Uncle Alex would have done, and she was even more gratified when George returned with eyes wide as saucers.

Once seated, he looked at her furtively before leaning close and whispering. "Did you see the size of those paw prints?"

She said not a word, only nodding knowingly at him. Without any further argument, George cleaned his plate, then asked for seconds. He gulped down the last bite and urgently rose. "I'll be right back, Penelope. Wait here."

As soon as he left, Nurse Sasha sat down across from Penelope and placed the kettle down on the table between them. "That was awfully kind of you, Penelope. Here's a warm cup of tea for you. Your hands must be freezing after drawing those paw prints in all that snow."

"My hands are perfectly fine," Penelope replied, holding out a hand,

Nurse Sasha took Penelope's hand in her own and was startled to find that it was, in fact, warm. She stared wonderingly at the girl but had no time to press her for answers, for at just that moment, George came bursting in, dressed for a long trek in the snow.

Penelope Grace grinned. The search for the great Wilderbeast was about to begin.

They raced down the snow-covered steps, each eager to catch their first glimpse of the Wilderbeast.

"Where should we look first?" George asked, his face vibrant with anticipation and joy.

"Well, she came up our steps from the right, so —"

"To the park! Race you!"

Penelope laughed and ran after him, her cloak flowing behind her as she hurried to catch up.

They were nearly there when George finally slowed, his cheeks bright pink from the cold. "Do you suppose, Penelope," he asked in between deep breaths, "that the Wilderbeast will hurt us?"

"Never! Wilderbeasts come to the brave of heart to take them on wild adventures. They would never hurt anyone."

With the park now in view, she smiled and cried, "Come on!"

Both Penelope and George quickly lost track of time and the Wilderbeast, but their time in the park did them immeasurable good. For a while, they could remember that, despite their concerns, there was still hope if they would only look for it.

Sometime later, as they made their way home, Penelope felt all the more determined to help her father; she could see him failing, could see all his joy and warmth fading in time with Uncle Alex. Perhaps, this Christmas would not be the same, but Penelope Grace fiercely believed that it could still be good.

Only a few streets separated them from home when George, suddenly remembering, cried in dismay, "The Wilderbeast! We never found her!"

"It will be all right, George. You never know when she might appear."

They spent the next several minutes debating with great animation what the Wilderbeast might look like. As they turned down their street, George stopped in his tracks, delighted that they no longer had to guess.

Halfway down the street, just a few feet from their doorstep, the Wilderbeast lay settled in the snow, as if waiting for them all this time. She looked very much like a dragon, but rather than scales, her sleek frame was covered in fur of a soft violet color, dappled in blue and green. As Penelope and George drew near, the Wilderbeast rose, extending her gossamer wings and lowering her head to look at them with her great, green eyes, the color of moss on rain-soaked bark.

They were less than a hundred yards from her when George halted, looking up at the Wilderbeast in wonder. "She looks so kind," he breathed.

"That's so those who look closely enough will know they don't have to be afraid of her."

He was quiet for a moment more, then, "What's her name?"

"Lunella," Penelope replied, "for the way her wings shimmer in the moonlight."

Just then, the Wilderbeast, seeming to decide that the two were worthy companions, lay on the ground once more and extended her leg so that Penelope and George could climb up.

"Shall we get on?" Penelope asked.

George offered her nothing more than a smile for an answer, and together, they ran to the Wilderbeast, but then –

"What on earth are you doing?"

Their father stood on the doorstep, and the Wilderbeast disappeared like a dusting of snow snatched by an icy breeze.

"We were playing," Penelope answered.

Their father said nothing for a moment, but both could feel his rage. "Your uncle is dying. Can you think of no better use for your time?"

Penelope was stunned by his anger, for all their games and imaginings had never brought him anything but joy, and she was suddenly angry, angry that he would seek to steal what relief she and George had found. "You never would have scolded us for something like this before!"

His tone still harsh, he retorted, "Things are different now, Penelope. Things are changing." And then, as if defeated by his own words, he hung his head, not even noticing the immense paw prints covering the steps.

Penelope and George said nothing, for they did not know what to say to this new version of their father. Words proved unnecessary.

"The doctor is here. Get inside," John said quietly, and Penelope and George, not wanting to upset him further, followed him through the door.

Penelope Grace sat close beside her father, but she had never felt more separate from him. Dr. Wilbourne had left them moments before, promising to return once he visited the other patients who had been waiting for him. He had not left them with good news.

He could do nothing for Uncle Alex and had only left them with the charge to continue watching over him and to keep him comfortable. None of them had ever felt so helpless, save John. He could flawlessly recall being four years old, refusing to listen to his mother as she tried to tell him that his father, George, was dead. He could imagine himself on the day of the funeral, rooted to the third step up, looking out the front windows as his uncles carried his father's casket to the waiting hearse.

John had not felt so helpless since, and the memories of that time, coupled with the fear of more loss, made him unbearably angry. Why should he be forced to lose another father? Why should he be forced to feel how powerless he was? Yet he did not voice these questions, though his family could guess what he was feeling, and he did not look for comfort from them, though they were longing to give it.

Penelope, knowing she could not force her father to accept help, turned her attention to Uncle Alex. She knelt by his side, tenderly holding his hand in her own. She said nothing at first, only sat and watched him, hoping to memorize the lines on his face.

The thought of losing him terrified Penelope, and the idea that she might never again see such a beloved face absolutely baffled her, yet she could not forget his words to her by the fire that night. To surrender her sense of wonder would be to do precisely what Uncle Alex had warned her against, and so she was determined to hold tightly to wonder and help her family do the same.

Carefully now, Penelope placed her hand upon his cheek and whispered, "I love you."

Though he could no longer answer her, she could feel all the fierceness of love returned in full, and she smiled in spite of her pain. At that moment, and much to Penelope's surprise, her father knelt on the carpet beside her.

He said nothing for several long moments, then, as if voicing his thoughts to no one in particular, he muttered, "To think that he might soon be gone."

Tentatively, Penelope Grace put her hand on her father's arm. "I'm scared to lose him, too, Papa." She paused, hesitant to say what she felt she must. "I believe that, even though we are hurting, Uncle Alex would want us to remember that our time with him has been so good."

"Yes," he said, rising abruptly, "but not enough."

Penelope looked up at him, startled by the hard, bitter edge to his voice. Her words had managed to shake him free of his thoughts, yes, but they had done nothing to loosen his grip on anger and fear. She looked to her mother for help as he stalked away, but Mary knew they must let him grieve in his own way and do their best to remind him that he was not alone.

Disheartened, Penelope left the room. For the next several hours, she alternated between aimlessly searching for household chores that would keep her hands busy and anxiously keeping watch at Uncle Alex's side. But the tension in the room kept building as the day dragged on and they watched Uncle Alex's breathing worsen, and Penelope, feeling that she must escape it for a while, rose quickly and went to the kitchen.

Nurse Sasha greeted her with a comforting hand on her shoulder and a cup of tea. It grew cool in Penelope's hands as she thought about her father and how she could help him. She had many ideas but wondered if any of them would work or if he would reject them as he had her efforts to comfort and encourage Georgie.

But Penelope could think about it no more as Georgie's sobs broke through her thoughts. Without hesitation, she ran from the room, heedless of the teacup rolling across the kitchen floor.

She stopped short just outside the doorway, frightened of confronting what would inevitably become real once she stepped across the threshold. Yet, as Penelope Grace looked at her family kneeling together beside Uncle Alex's still frame, it seemed to her that a shadow began to darken above her father's shoulders, threatening to lay claim to her mother and Georgie as well.

She hurried to them. Georgie, still holding tightly to their mother's hand, climbed into Penelope's lap as she laid her head on her father's shoulder. For a little while, they remained that way, unquestionably in pain, but not alone.

But this closeness did not last. Penelope watched, helpless, while her father spiraled through the rest of the night's events. The doctor returned, the death certificate was signed – a problem of the heart cited as the cause of death – and Uncle Alex's body was taken away.

The house felt empty, and they all sat, numb to the sudden cold.

Yet, as the initial shock slowly began to fade, Penelope could feel her father's anger building again, and, unable to face it, she retreated to her room, though she knew she would not sleep.

Curled up in a blanket, Penelope Grace sat on the window seat for a while, watching the snow swirl across their quiet street. Tomorrow was Christmas Eve, but instead of approaching it with her usual anticipation, she feared what the morning might bring.

She woke to find that she had fallen asleep on the window seat. For several minutes, she did not move but remained where she was, taking several deep breaths as she came to terms with the knowledge that Uncle Alex was gone.

Opening her eyes once more, Penelope Grace watched the snow coming to cover the earth, comforted by the familiar stillness and quiet of snow falling. But she could not stay here. Little as she wanted to confront her father's anger or Uncle Alex's empty chair, Penelope knew she must. And though none of them much felt like celebrating, Penelope believed she must do what she could to make it feel at least a little like Christmas for Georgie.

Penelope walked down the hallway and was greeted by the sound of the usual hustle and bustle of Christmas Eve floating up the stairs. She stopped, uncertain. Angry and hurt as her father was, Penelope could not believe that he had decided to continue with their usual festivities. But Penelope Grace dared to hope.

Halfway down the stairs, she was unkindly met by the swift and sudden shock of disappointment. Her mother and Nurse Sasha, both with heads down, were removing the last of the greenery from the banister. Her father stood near the Christmas tree, which looked stark and out of place without its ornaments, and Georgie went about the room, collecting all the candles before dropping them in a box at their father's feet.

John reached up to remove the candles from the tree. Penelope, frozen on the steps until now, rushed down them, desperate to put a stop to this. "Papa, please," she cried, holding tightly to his arm, "not the candles!"

"Penelope, stop," he replied. "I have a funeral to arrange. I do not need to be constantly reminded that this Christmas, and every one after, will be spent without him."

"But Papa, we need the light," she insisted, forcing herself between her father and the tree.

"I said no," he shouted with all the force of his anger.

Suddenly, Penelope took a sharp gasp in, stumbling back into the tree in her fright. Behind her father loomed a horrible figure, his face pale and drawn, but his smile wicked.

"P-papa, behind you," she barely stammered out.

He looked over his shoulder and saw nothing. When he turned back and spoke, his voice was quiet but barely controlled. "Penelope, these childish imaginings must stop."

Incredulous, she cried, "What? I would not lie about something like this! Can't you see him?"

"That's enough," John roared. He was silent for a few sharp breaths. "You will take down the candles," he said and turned away from Penelope.

As the figure behind him passed by, he would not take his eyes off of Penelope Grace. He looked triumphant. She watched, sickened and scared, as he followed closely behind her father, clinging to him like an oily shadow.

Once alone, Penelope Grace took several deep breaths to steady herself, then bent down to pick up the candles she had knocked off the tree in her fright. Her hands were still shaking.

All the same, she reached for the last candle, which had rolled beneath the tree. As she did so, Penelope noticed a small box tucked between the presents her father had yet to carry away. It was wrapped in gold paper with cream-colored string and easily fit in the palm of her hand. Penelope could not have said what made her so sure that it was meant for her, but as she untied the string and lifted the lid, she was proven right.

A note folded into a tight square lay just inside. Penelope carefully unfolded it and was comforted by the sight of Uncle Alex's familiar writing, thankful for the gift of feeling, if only for a few moments, that he was somehow still there.

She read the note slowly, savoring his words.

My sweetest Penelope Grace,

Your grandmother asked me to give this to you. Her child-like spirit shone like a bright light within. May yours always do the same.

With love,
Uncle Alex

Placing the note in her lap, Penelope gingerly lifted a locket out of the box. It was a faded gold and had beautiful etching on the front. A short length of chain led to three small, golden roses, which attached the locket to the rest of the long chain.

Penelope Grace put the necklace round her neck; it hung nearly to her waist. Finding the latch, she pressed it and jumped slightly as three metal plates popped out. Including the locket's case, there were five in all. Each was curved around the edges as if meant to hold the smallest of pictures. All of the plates were the same beautiful, faded gold, but they were all of them empty. But that made no sense. Penelope Grace wondered why her grandmother had felt it was so important to give her an empty locket.

She could not puzzle it out. Setting aside the mystery, for the time being, Penelope closed the locket and reached under the tree for the gift that she and Uncle Alex had made for Georgie.

She found her little brother sitting on the floor of his room, surrounded by his usual mess of toys and playing with none of them. Penelope sat beside him, saying nothing, and handed him the gift. At first, she wondered if he would even open it, but at last, he began to tear at the paper. His eyes grew wide as he pulled out a wooden sword, polished to a beautiful gleam, its pommel and blade carved with intricate engravings.

His whole face lit up with joy, and Penelope grinned, so relieved was she to see him smile.

"Uncle Alex and I felt it was only right for Sir George to have a proper blade," Penelope explained excitedly. "Uncle Alex started on the carving months ago. He taught me how, and I helped with some of it."

But even as she spoke, George's face fell. "It's not real, Penelope."

"What?"

"They're just stories, Penelope. None of it's real."

She did not know what to say, and George, setting the sword aside, left the room before she could find the right words.

The next two days passed mostly in silence. The funeral arrangements were quickly made, condolences offered, and the Christmas decorations stowed away.

Penelope watched as her father's anger consumed him and steadily stole the life from her mother as every effort Mary made to comfort her husband failed. The despair in the house was crippling, and they were all of them stumbling beneath the weight of it. Penelope tried everything she could think of, but the distance between them kept growing, and she could find no way of closing it.

On the evening after the funeral, she sat crying in her room, longing for the familiar comfort of the holiday lights, though Penelope Grace knew that, even had her father allowed the candles to remain, the house still would have felt dark.

Part Two: Winter

Wonder, at its strongest, will always attract the attention of those who fear it and wish to destroy it.

Denagon was one such being. He had only ever understood pride and greed and the selfish taking of what belongs to others. His fate was decided from the beginning, yet his destructive work never ceased.

He watched her now as she cried late into the night, pathetic and alone. He hated the light she carried, hated the way it spread to everyone whose life she touched. But if he was skilled at anything, it was at separating one from another. Denagon slid from the room in the company of deep shadow to find Penelope's father, whose light would be the first to fail.

John sat facing the window, keenly aware of the empty space behind him. He had grown so used to having Uncle Alex with them. Nine years had passed since the day his uncle had arrived from Nysiros. John had become frighteningly comfortable in the certainty that when he entered the family room or sat down to dinner, Uncle Alex would be there.

He was a fool to have thought it would last forever.

Absentmindedly, he ran his fingers across the black fabric band tied around his upper left arm, a Greek tradition that honored the loss of family and friends.

Time was a relentless march, John knew, yet as he peered out the frost-covered window, he could not help but feel that everything had gone terribly still. He dreaded the long stretch of winter.

Once, the coming of this season held as much anticipation for him as the holidays, but John could not manufacture the feeling this year. The hope of Christmas had soured for him, and the vast expanse of long, cold hours he would spend trapped in a house that endlessly reminded him of Uncle Alex held no charm.

John's thoughts briefly turned to Penelope. He knew what his darling girl wanted from him, and he could not give it. Everything felt dark and unchanging, and he could not pretend to believe in hope when he could no longer see it.

Mary wrapped her arms around John, startling him as she did so. "Darling, come and be with us. The children are missing you."

He shifted away from her touch, uncomfortable with her request. "No, Mary. I would like to be left alone."

But she would not relent, though she remained gentle in her encouragement. "It would do us all good to be together, John." She added quietly, "We are all hurting."

"Am I selfish then?" he challenged, recoiling from her.

"John —."

"Leave me be. I'm no fit company tonight."

Reluctantly, she pulled away from him, hesitant to leave, though she knew he did not want her. As she returned to their children, Mary's heart broke to see the first hopeful smile she had seen on George's face in days slowly fade.

Knowing the answer, he still asked, "Is Papa coming?"

"No, George, he is not."

Mary watched as a cloud of hurt masked her youngest's usually joyful expression; she felt so utterly helpless, for she could not make his father behave any differently, and she was losing the energy to continue trying. Before she could conjure up anything remotely comforting to say, George stormed up the stairs. Mary stood in the middle of the room, feeling lost. A soft touch on her arm jolted her back to the present moment.

"It will be all right, Mama," Penelope said. "Please stay. Maybe we can convince Papa to change his mind."

At the thought, Mary felt suddenly tired. All she wanted was to lie down. "Another night, Penelope. Perhaps it was too soon to try."

And with that, she, too, retreated upstairs.

She kept hoping her mother would turn around or that Georgie would return to the family room, ready to plead with their father once more with his usual mischievous grin.

No one appeared.

Penelope Grace, now alone with her father, summoned up her remaining courage and went to him. His back faced the rest of the room, and she nearly lost her nerve but made herself speak in the end.

"Papa, would you sit with me awhile?"

He did not stir.

"Papa?"

She waited a few moments for his response, though it hurt her to know how oblivious he was to her. When it was long past obvious that she would get no answer from her father tonight, Penelope, at last, followed in Georgie's and her mother's footsteps.

She stopped at the foot of the staircase when a faint touch of frigid air swept past her. The cold never troubled Penelope Grace, but it was unnatural to feel its touch indoors. Wondering at the cause of it, Penelope searched the lower half of the house for an improperly latched window but found no such thing.

Frowning at the unwelcome mystery, she returned to the stairs, troubled, but at a loss for any sort of explanation. For every step Penelope Grace took, the air grew colder. Halfway up, she snatched her hand back from the banister with a sharp intake of breath. The light was dim, but she could still make out a small patch of ice, which was slowly expanding to cover the length of the polished wood. Penelope stepped back, frightened and confused by what was happening. Her breath came in visible, panicked gasps as she rushed up the last of the stairs, the only way she could think of to escape the cold and ice.

Escape is rarely so simple.

A fresh gust of wind struck Penelope just as she reached the landing. Her eyes widening in horror, she barely succeeded in stifling a cry as she watched frost begin to curl its way around the pattern on the wallpaper. It was the first time that Penelope remembered thinking of ice as something cruel.

As Penelope sought to understand what was happening, her thoughts inevitably turned to the pale figure she had seen bearing down on her father. She did not know who or what he was, but she could not shake the growing conviction that he was the source of this strange attack on her family.

The frost, at last, slowed to a stop, but Penelope Grace felt no comfort in that; there was simply nothing left for it to claim. She stood in the chill space, wondering how long it would take for the ice to cover the rest of her home, and if it would stop there.

"Is something the matter, Penelope?"

She jumped at the unexpected sound. Turning to face Nurse Sasha, Penelope knew instantly that she could not see the frost encasing the walls and fought to hide her fear. "I'm all right, Nurse Sasha. I thought I saw something, but I was wrong."

Though Penelope's reassurance was less than convincing, Nurse Sasha only nodded and began to go down the steps. But Penelope stopped her, frowning at the bundle in her arms.

"Are those Uncle Alex's things?"

"Your father wants his room emptied," she answered, clearly uncomfortable with the question.

Penelope's alarm flared. "We cannot act as if he were never here."

Nurse Sasha leveled a resigned gaze at her. "We might be better off if we tried."

Penelope was stunned by her words, but even had she been able to think of a good response, Nurse Sasha gave her no opportunity to offer one. Disheartened and exhausted, Penelope unwillingly followed her family's example and sought out the empty comfort of solitude.

The next day proved to be no better, and Penelope Grace grew increasingly desperate. Nurse Sasha went mindlessly about her work, Georgie could not be convinced to play, and her parents only retreated further into themselves. All the while, Penelope watched the ice and bitter cold steal through the house. There had been no sign of the figure haunting her family, though she looked for evidence of his presence.

Nevertheless, the unnatural cold encasing the house was enough to convince Penelope Grace that he was hanging over their home like a persistent shadow. Yet, even were he to appear, Penelope had no clue how she would fight him or keep him from harming her family. She did not even understand what he was or what kind of threat he posed. How do you fight something you don't understand?

All Penelope knew was that her family was deteriorating, and she was faltering beneath the weight of trying to make them well again. George hardly spoke two words to her and had refused her hopeful suggestion that they go outside to search for the Wilderbeast once again.

More painful than that, however, was watching her mother reach out to Papa, determined to love him through the worst of days, and be rejected at every turn. With every attempt, her father only grew angrier, and Penelope spent the day in dread of his temper.

Though this side of her father was strange to her, she understood enough to know that a time would come when he could no longer hold his anger in check. Penelope felt as though she was holding her breath, waiting for the horrible moment to arrive.

The long-expected shouts drew her attention just before dinner, and Penelope rushed to the dining room. Georgie stood just outside, crying as their parents fought. She had never seen him look so frightened.

When he saw Penelope, he ran to her. "Please make them stop, Penelope!"

She held him tightly for a moment, wishing she could do as he asked, but unsure how. As their parents' shouts grew louder, though, Penelope Grace knew she must try. Uncertain as she was, she entered the room.

Mary was trying to draw close to John, but he took several steps away from her. "I only want to help you, John," Mary cried.

"I do not *want* to feel better, Mary! And by trying to force me to, you only make things worse! Can you not see that?"

Mary looked as if she had been forcefully struck by his words. Penelope could not stand to see her hurting so, and she came forward, determined to say what was in her heart. But her father anticipated her and, wanting no part of it, retreated from the room.

Penelope Grace would not be deterred. "Papa," she shouted as she followed him into the family room.

A thin layer of frost was beginning to cover the walls as they entered, and it seemed to Penelope that the light of the fire was growing dim. A sense of urgency gripped her.

She reached out to hold her father's hand. "Papa, please stop this. I know we all miss Uncle Alex, but he would not want this. He would want us to remember that there is still reason to hope."

He snatched his hand away from her and slammed it down on a side table. "If there is hope, why did He take Uncle Alex from us? Why did He not make him well?" John demanded, his voice quavering.

"I don't know," Penelope cried. "I just believe He's still good!"

At her words, John suddenly seemed very small. "I can see no goodness in this," he whispered.

And just like that, all her frustration faded, and Penelope Grace's heart ached for her father. John stared into the fire for several breaths.

"Papa..." Penelope ventured.

He looked up at her, but he still seemed far off. "Go to bed, Penelope. Take George upstairs as well."

"But Papa —"

"Go," he said, his voice quiet but unyielding.

She knew that pressing him further would only lead to more unrest, and so she went upstairs with two plates and ate a silent meal with Georgie before tucking him into bed.

A few minutes later, Penelope Grace sat on the window seat in her room — a nightly tradition now — and held on to the chain around her neck, wishing that her grandmother had chosen to leave her something more than an empty locket.

Georgie's panicked cries woke her with a start. Penelope rushed into the hallway, only to be met by a gust of frigid air. The banister was slick with ice and offered no support as she raced down the stairs. There was real anguish in Georgie's voice and real terror in Penelope's heart. She stopped in stunned disbelief just beyond the threshold.

Moonlight shone through the windows, causing every ice-encrusted surface to glitter and fill the room with a cold radiance. Near the long-dead fire, their Mama and Papa sat frozen, captive to the ice and cold. She ran to them, unable to stifle a ragged cry to see the way her Mama's arms were held tightly around Papa like a shield that, for all its determination and strength, had not been enough to save him.

George shook them frantically, crying for them to wake, but Penelope knew they would not.

They had to get out.

Whoever their enemy was, she knew from the prickle of her skin that he was here, though she could not see him. Penelope reached for Georgie, but just as she did, a horrified shout sounded behind them.

Penelope jerked sharply around. Nurse Sasha was stumbling back, visibly shaken by what she was seeing. Their enemy stood behind her.

"Nurse Sasha, stop!"

But no sooner did the words fly from her lips than their kind friend collapsed into the figure's waiting arms. Penelope Grace rushed forward, heedless of the danger, desperate to save Nurse Sasha if she could, while their enemy circled her and Georgie in his wicked hunt.

The cold of Nurse Sasha's skin seemed to burn Penelope's hand, but she stubbornly held on all the same. She had gone terribly pale, and Penelope could see the warmth leaving her.

"What's happening?" Nurse Sasha managed to whisper.

"I don't know, but please stay with us," Penelope pleaded.

Nurse Sasha trembled violently until she went numb to the cold and was still. Penelope watched in horror as the ice claimed her. But there was no time to try to help her or their parents, no time to wonder or understand what was happening. She had to keep Georgie safe.

Penelope turned around to find her little brother face to face with their enemy, whose empty eyes were locked on his. Georgie was frozen in fear, desperate to flee, but unable to.

Frightened as she was, Penelope Grace would not allow her brother to be taken. She grabbed Georgie's hand. "Run with me, Georgie!"

They fled up the stairs, Penelope helping Georgie as he struggled on the icy surface. In moments, they were huddled on the floor, hiding behind a locked door that she felt certain could not protect them.

She did not know what else to do.

She had to keep Georgie safe, yet he was already trembling much as Nurse Sasha had. Penelope Grace moved closer to him and held his hands tightly in her own.

"Georgie, I know this is frightening, but we have to be brave," she said, fondly brushing the hair from his eyes. "Like St. George."

But he shook his head even as she spoke. "I'm not big enough, Penelope."

She nearly lost her nerve when she noticed that his lips were turning blue, but she would not give up. "Your heart is plenty big enough, Georgie," she replied.

But no matter how fiercely Penelope Grace believed this, she could not make him feel the same. Ice began to coat the walls and floor. Her heart was in her throat when she saw the figure on the far side of her room, making his inevitable way to Georgie. Though he was just as pale as the first time she saw him, he seemed stronger and terribly assured of his victory.

"Georgie, look at me," Penelope pleaded, trying to sound unafraid, though she could hear the panic in her voice. "You have to fight this, Georgie."

He shook his head, the cold making his movements sluggish and awkward. She gripped his hand harder as if, through the sheer force of her own will, she could keep him from falling into their enemy's trap.

He drew closer to Georgie, his shadow lengthening as he stretched out his hand. Penelope felt a rush of indignation and love, and without thinking, she roughly shoved the pale hand from her brother's shoulder. "Keep away from him!"

Denagon hissed, retreating from the sudden, radiant light that illuminated the room. He seemed to shrink in the presence of its brilliance, but before Penelope could comprehend what was happening, he fled.

But all she cared for at that moment was Georgie. Penelope Grace cradled her little brother in her arms, willing her own warmth to fill him. He would not wake, and she wept as she rocked back and forth, holding her little brother, unwilling to let him go.

But she could not stay like this forever. Already, Penelope could feel the chill from his cold frame seeping into her own body and, horrified by the thought, she stood up, staggering as she retreated from him.

Penelope Grace sat in the farthest corner of the window seat, knees to chest, trying to make her hands stop shaking. The loss of everyone she loved most was more than she could bear or understand. She sat, curled up by the window, her ragged cries the only sound in the horribly still house.

"Help me," she whimpered. "Please help me."

Nothing happened that she could see, and she remained where she was, her cries gradually quieting. When, at last, Penelope Grace fell silent, renewed fear gripped her. Someone was watching her.

She looked up sharply and searched the room, but no one was there. Yet, the feeling persisted. She sat patiently, sure that her family's attacker would appear at any time, but the room remained empty, save for her, and Georgie's still frame.

Hesitantly, she turned her back on the room and looked out the window.

A sharp gasp escaped her.

Standing in the middle of the snow-covered street, looking up at her, was a white wolf.

Aira knew the girl in the window was the one meant to follow, for this is where the Wind led her. She stood patiently, her paws sinking into the deepening snow, as the girl stared and wondered.

Aira knew that she was the one meant to follow, but would she?

Penelope Grace did not move for several seconds, but eventually, curiosity got the better of her, and she leaned forward, pressing her cold fingertips against the glass. The wolf perked up at this and, confident that it had her attention, ran down the street.

Penelope only sat and watched the creature disappear from sight, feeling oddly lonesome at its absence. But before she could, once again, feel her solitude so keenly, the wolf returned. Once again, it stood in the middle of the street, panting now, its breath visible in the frigid night air.

She rose, leaning on her knees now, and watched the wolf intently. Again, the wolf ran down the street, only to return and watch Penelope with an expectant gaze. Penelope Grace could hardly allow herself to understand the wolf's meaning.

It wanted her to follow.

But why? And to where?

Believing that a wolf wanted her to follow it through a frost-laden night was illogical at best. Thinking that a wolf was the response to her desperate plea seemed even worse.

Yet, she had asked for help, and who was she to question the answer she received?

There was no one left in the house to offer their advice, and Penelope Grace found that she was altogether willing to embrace this entirely child-like and impossible hope.

The wolf was running again, and she knew in her heart that it was not coming back. There was no time left to think or question. She ran to her brother and tenderly lifted him onto the bed, promising him that she would be back, and she would find a way to save their family. Penelope retrieved her boots and soft pink, velvet cloak from her armoire, and rushed downstairs.

As she stepped out into the bitter cold, she could see no sign of the wolf at first. She walked down the street, the gas lamps her only source of light, following the wolf's paw prints. A few moments later, she could see the wolf standing beneath the last light on the street, waiting for her.

At the sight of the girl, the wolf ran, and Penelope Grace chased this unexpected friend through the dark night and the thickly falling snow.

With each step, Penelope Grace sank into the powdery, wet snow blanketing the park. The wolf had slowed once they reached the park, allowing Penelope a chance to catch her breath as she followed, undaunted by the cold.

Tall trees towered above them on either side, and she soon realized that this was farther than she and Georgie had ever ventured into the park's forest. The trees were closer together here, and as she walked with the wolf beneath their ice-laden boughs, Penelope Grace felt as though she were being enveloped by an altogether different world.

Several more minutes passed, and they reached a bend in the park's path, marking the point where travelers could circle back to the park's entrance. Penelope continued on for a few steps before realizing that the wolf was standing still several paces behind her.

She stared at the wolf, curious. "Where do you mean for us to go?" she asked, half expecting the wolf to answer.

The wolf only stared back, patiently waiting for her to understand its meaning. Penelope moved to stand beside the wolf, and the creature nudged her hand before gazing toward an unremarkable break in the trees just off the path. Penelope understood. The wolf meant for her to leave the path and enter the forest, but she was hesitant to wander through such an unfamiliar place.

But what else could she do? She had traveled this far, and there was no hope to be found for her family if she turned back. With a deep breath, Penelope Grace ducked beneath the lowest-hanging branches and stepped into the forest. It was not long before she realized that they were, indeed, still following a path. Though it was worn and covered in thick patches of ice and snow, it was there, and it offered Penelope a measure of comfort.

The wolf followed faithfully behind, watchful for any danger. But they were alone in this winter forest, and Penelope and the wolf continued on quietly, both understanding that the silence of this place was sacred and worth leaving undisturbed. They walked in this way for some time, until, all of a sudden, the wolf trotted ahead of her.

Penelope could feel the creature's expectation fill her as well, and her heart began to beat faster as they approached a clearing in the forest. Without warning, the wolf ran forward, gracefully maneuvering the small gap in the trees that marked the entrance to the clearing, and Penelope followed suit. Gently pushing aside the branches of an evergreen, Penelope Grace stepped into the clearing and found that she could not take another step. She was stunned and enchanted.

On the opposite side of the clearing stood an ice-blue carousel, covered in snow.

She could see from this distance that ice had coated the carousel's gleaming silver poles, while patches of snow disguised the carousel's animals. Only the moonlight illuminated it, setting countless glittering snowflakes ablaze, and Penelope Grace admired its reflected light. The carousel looked as if it had been forgotten for a hundred endless winters until the ice and snow had come to cover it and claim the carousel for its own. Almost, it seemed wrong to do anything but leave it untouched.

The wolf thought otherwise. It came to stand behind Penelope and nudged her forward. Hesitantly, she followed the wolf's lead, but her curiosity and wonder were such that she no longer needed much encouragement to explore. She climbed the silver steps that led up to the carousel and stood, transfixed. Each silver and ice-blue surface was decorated with the most beautiful etching that Penelope had ever seen. Looking around, she was convinced of the care that had gone into crafting the carousel.

Penelope stepped carefully on the carousel's platform as she admired its animal figures, both familiar and fantastic alike. There were horses painted in brilliant, wintry hues, and in front of them pranced a white unicorn, pure and exultant as it led the carousel's procession.

Next, followed a family of polar bears — a mother and two cubs — and a noble creature that looked suspiciously similar to the Wilderbeast. Penelope smiled at the reminder of her adventures with Georgie as she continued to walk around the carousel and passed by a white lion, fierce and powerful, and a white tiger, its black stripes gleaming against the white of its fur.

At last, she had circled around to the front of the carousel, and there was only one carved animal remaining: a white wolf. Penelope Grace stopped short before looking over to the wolf, standing patiently at the foot of the carousel's steps. It stared back at her, its gaze inscrutable. Gingerly, Penelope dusted the snow off of the wolf figure's face, revealing the same kind, intelligent eyes. The figure and the wolf who had led her here were a perfect match.

Curious, she thought. It was then that she noticed another figure peeking out from behind the wolf's legs. She bent down to find an intricately carved arctic fox and wondered what its story might be.

After another moment, Penelope rose and looked down at the wolf, who stood beside her now. Again, the creature nudged her hand, directing her with a look toward the center of the carousel. In the carousel's central pillar, at eye level, was what Penelope took to be a keyhole, though it was unlike any that she had ever seen. It was in the shape of five perfect circles, shaped rather like a star.

The keyhole was strange, true, but it did not remain a mystery to Penelope for long. Carefully now, she removed the locket that Uncle Alex had given her from around her neck and pressed the latch. Five perfectly round plates revealed themselves, and she understood at last why her grandmother had seen fit to give her an empty locket.

She walked forward, her hands almost shaking with anticipation, and pressed the locket into the keyhole with a soft snap. Like her, reader, you will not be disappointed by what happens next.

Softly at first, Penelope Grace heard a melody — one of those beautiful melodies that make you think of all things quiet and good.

The carousel flared to life and began to turn. Penelope took hold of one of the silver poles and leaned against the unicorn, uncertain of what to expect. Beyond the carousel, the wind began to pick up, lifting the falling snow along with it in a great swirl that enveloped the turning carousel. The music grew louder, and the wind increased to a gale until all Penelope could hear and see was a beautiful melody and swirling snow.

Had you entered the clearing only moments later, you would have found that the winter carousel was gone and Penelope Grace with it.

Slowly, the melody faded, the snow cleared, and the carousel was still. Penelope Grace looked around, breathless. They were in a forest still, but no forest that she had ever wandered in. These trees were tall and almost silver to her eyes, with deep green leaves edged with crisp snow.

She stepped down from the carousel, longing to take in every detail of this beautiful place. The ground beneath her feet was covered in a thin layer of snow, but patches of green were still visible, and when she looked more closely, she noticed something unusual. All across the clearing, thin tendrils of ice had grown and curved to form intricate frost flowers that glimmered in the starlight. Penelope turned slowly, feeling as though she were standing on a carpet of frosted lace.

But a rustle in the forest alerted her, pulling her away from her admiration of this new place. Penelope was acutely aware of how quiet the forest was. Though the woods near her home was also very still, this silence felt watchful and made Penelope nervous. She turned to find the wolf still standing faithfully behind her, its eyes fixed on the clearing's edge. Penelope peered into the dark space between the trees but could see nothing.

Then, a whisper of a voice behind her.

Penelope whirled around. For all her courage, she was growing frightened. "Who's there?" she asked sharply.

A large shape lumbered through the trees in front of her. Penelope backed away until she felt the wolf's fur against her hands. A moment later, an enormous polar bear stepped into the clearing, followed closely by two cubs.

Penelope Grace's breathing quickened, and she could feel the quick sharpness of panic welling up. But before she could make any move to flee, the forest was full of the rustling of movement, and as she spun around, more animals joined the polar bears around the edge of the clearing.

Several deer were peeking tentatively around the edge of the carousel, and three horses trotted to stand nearby with their graceful heads held high. While these did nothing to inspire fear in Penelope's heart, the other creatures were an entirely different matter.

Penelope watched with bated breath as a white tiger emerged from the forest, its blue eyes fixed on her. Directly to the tiger's left, a large white lion stepped out of the tree's shadows, and Penelope trembled at the sound of the rumble at the back of its throat. Quickly, she contemplated how she might flee from these powerful creatures, but could think of nothing. She did not have the strength to outrun them.

Still, she must try. But just as she made to escape, a voice sounded beside her.

"All is well."

She froze. Sure of what she had heard, still, she could scarcely believe it. She looked down at her companion.

"They will not harm you."

The voice had come from the wolf.

Now, Penelope Grace was a lover of stories, and all things considered fantastic and seemingly impossible, but even she, full of wonder, was taken aback by this. She could form no words, and the wolf waited, patient as always.

Several seconds passed before she succeeded in stuttering out, "You can talk!" Hardly the most imaginative reply, but it was the best her stunned mind could manage.

But before the wolf could answer her, an arctic fox entered the clearing. "Aye, we all can," the fox bluntly stated as it trotted forward to stand in front of Penelope.

"Tilly," the wolf growled, a warning in its voice.

"Oh, hush, Aira! She might as well get used to it." Tilly turned an expectant gaze on Penelope. "*Are* ye used to it?"

Despite her shock, Penelope Grace nearly laughed at Tilly's brusqueness, but a look from the fox made her think better of it, and she simply answered, "Yes," though she questioned if that were true.

"Good. Let's get on with things then," Tilly replied, and disappeared back into the forest, the rest of her companions leaping through the snow after her.

Penelope stood there, bewildered, having hoped for a little more explanation than that.

A rumble of what was clearly laughter escaped from the lion. "Come along, child. You'll learn to humor Tilly before long."

The other animals had already followed after the fox, but the tiger and lion waited at the clearing's edge for Penelope and Aira. As the girl and wolf passed beneath the trees, the cats came along either side of them, like sentinels guarding them against any danger biding its time in the shadows.

As they ventured deeper into the forest, Penelope Grace grew increasingly uneasy. The carousel's clearing had felt enchanted and sheltered, but here, Penelope felt entirely exposed even with the closeness of the trees.

The flutter of wings momentarily distracted her, and Penelope Grace looked up as a brilliantly red cardinal came to rest on a low-hanging branch not far above Aira's watchful gaze. The wolf halted, listening intently as the bird's melody filled the forest. Penelope gasped in surprise as she watched the bird, for as it sang, a swirling puff of air flowed from its beak, giving form to its song, like a melody made visible.

Her delight was swiftly cut short, however, as Aira delivered the bird's message to the waiting company. Something waited for them in this part of the forest, something that took particular interest in the presence of the girl.

Still, there was nothing for them to do but continue on, despite the risk. Penelope moved closer to Aira, feeling a measure of safety when she was next to the wolf, though she grew increasingly convinced that whatever waited for them was getting closer.

The further they walked, the deeper her creeping suspicion grew until all the hairs on the back of her neck stood on end. She thought of the pale figure haunting her family and stopped short. As she did, a dark figure shot across the path in front of them, disappearing just as quickly. Penelope gasped as the white tiger shot through the trees, growling with a menace that made her shudder, even though the tiger was her protector.

"Aira, is it him?" she asked, and the wolf knew instantly whom she meant.

"No, girl. Denagon is far from this place. But he has many helpers, many who will watch your movements through our land. He will know you are here soon."

Penelope let out a shaky breath, but before she could voice her panic, Aira nudged her hand. "We will keep you safe. But we must move."

Nodding her understanding, Penelope hurried to keep pace with Aira and the lion as they increased their speed. The trees began to grow further apart, and it was not long until they came upon a small camp where a number of the animals from the clearing had gathered. To the right of the gathering, Penelope was surprised to see a swift river flowing, untouched by the frozen world surrounding it. Upon noticing it, she realized with a start that, since entering this strange world, she had not felt the slightest shiver of cold. She felt her hands, and they were perfectly warm.

She was just about to ask Aira about it when the white tiger joined them, panting hard as it collapsed onto the snowy ground. "The beast escaped me, but it is gone. I'm sure I only encouraged it to warn Denagon sooner."

At this, Aira spoke up. "He would have learned of her soon enough, Copernicus. It is not your doing."

The tiger nodded his resignation. Penelope used the ensuing silence to ask her own questions, and they poured out one after another. "Is Denagon the figure who harmed my family? What is this place? How did you know I needed help?"

Tilly chuckled and answered with her own question. "What is yer name, child?"

"Penelope Grace. But please, help me understand."

"Yes, Penelope, Denagon is the one who attacked your family," Aira replied, her expression sad. "I knew to bring you to Ellura – our home – because the Wind led me to you."

"The Wind?"

But Aira would only say, "That is for another time."

Sensing that Aira would not change her mind, Penelope chose another question. "Why did Denagon attack us?"

Still, it was the wolf who answered. "All of us carry the mark of our Maker in our own way, but only humans were created to carry Apricity."

"What is Apricity?"

"You would best understand it as the warmth of the sun in winter," Copernicus answered this time, and Penelope heard the rumble of approval in the back of Aira's throat.

"Copernicus is right," Aira continued. "Apricity is the Light you carry, a Light that has been given. Denagon hates the Light, and he seeks to steal Apricity from all human souls. He has tried to do so since creation began, but he is growing more determined because he knows his time is short. You and your family carry Apricity, Penelope, and he wants nothing more than to take it from you."

"Is that what happened to them? But why?" she asked, shaking her head in confusion. "Why did he succeed with them and not me?"

"I do not have all the answers, Penelope Grace. What I do know is that you are a weaver of wonder, and you have been called to defend Apricity in the hearts of humans and help put a stop to Denagon's theft."

She grew quiet at the wolf's words. It seemed an impossible task, and she still didn't fully understand why she had been chosen or how she had arrived in this strange place. But she vividly remembered the sight and touch of everyone she loved, frozen and helpless at the hands of a wicked enemy.

"Are ye willin'?"

Tilly's question startled Penelope out of her thoughts, but she did not immediately answer. After a moment, she quietly asked, "Will it be dangerous?" though she knew the answer.

Tilly snorted. "Well, it certainly won't be safe." A determined, adventurous look filled the fox's eyes. "But it will be worth it to see yer family safe."

Penelope's eyes widened at the fox's words, for they reminded her of her own from a night not so long ago when she shared a tale of St. George with her little brother.

Again, Tilly broke into her thoughts. "I'll ask ye again. Are ye willin'?"

Penelope met Tilly's fierce gaze. She thought of the harm that had been done to her family and of the pain that might be inflicted on countless others if she did nothing, and Penelope Grace felt a fire building in her heart.

"Yes, I'm willing."

The white lion, Elafry, came to walk beside Penelope Grace as they traveled quickly through the forest. Dawn was beginning to filter through the trees, casting shadows that made her nervous, fearful of what might be hiding in them. Penelope shied away from the edges of the path.

Noticing her fear, Elafry spoke, startling Penelope from her thoughts. "My people are from this forest."

She looked over at him, intrigued despite her worries.

Encouraged by her interest, Elafry continued. "Many years ago, our leader, Brean, committed a terrible crime. He continued to lead us, but guilt consumed him. Our people extended forgiveness and welcomed his leadership; still, he could not shake it.

"One day, he left us, convinced that there could be no forgiveness for what he had done. Some little distance from here, he collapsed, crying out for relief, for some assurance that even he could be redeemed.

"He fell asleep, thinking he had received no answer. When next he woke, this forest had grown up around him, sheltering him. Eventually, our people found him, and we have lived here ever since. We call this forest Skia tou Eleos."

Penelope frowned, not understanding.

"Mercy's Shade," Elafry said softly.

Penelope smiled, feeling full and content at his words. She gave him an affectionate touch on his back and knew that she could now walk beneath these trees with less timidity. They continued in this way for several minutes before Penelope spoke again.

"Where is the polar bear leading us, Elafry?" she asked as her eyes traveled to the front of their company.

"That is Wynnfelde and her two cubs, Eloise and Frederick. She is taking us to the Ice Maiden," Elafry answered, and Penelope Grace could feel his joyful expectation.

"And she is?"

"You will see."

Penelope fell silent again, less than content with his response. Her hands trailed to her grandmother's locket, and she ventured another question. "Did you know my grandmother?"

A deep thrum sounded through Elafry. "Mary," he said, his voice warm and tender. "She was well-loved here."

Penelope Grace smiled, overjoyed that her grandmother was remembered with such affection. "How did she find this place, Elafry? Why did she leave me this locket? Did she know what would happen?"

"So many questions," Elafry replied with a rumbling chuckle. "I do not believe she knew what Denagon would do. Perhaps, she simply understood that one day, much like her, you would need to find a way into Ellura. It is no great surprise that she wanted to pass down to you the only way she knew of."

Penelope was undeterred. "You only answered two of my questions."

"The lion looked sidelong at her but did not give any sign of answering. After a few moments, Elafry said, "Much like the Wind, your grandmother's arrival in Ellura is a story for another night. And I believe it is not my story to tell."

She looked at Elafry curiously, wondering at the vagueness of his answer, but did not push him to explain.

Before another question could escape her, Aira padded through the crisp snow to walk beside her. "We are nearly there. Follow me closely, Penelope Grace."

Anticipation raced from one to the next, filling them all, making their steps quicken as they drew near to a frozen lake, quite different from the persistently running river that Penelope saw was its source. Perhaps a dozen feet separated the two bodies of water, and Penelope gasped in delight as she saw the rushing water transform into frozen rivulets that created a crystalline path to the lake. At the center of the lake, some four feet apart, were two beautiful swans, crafted from what looked to be blown glass.

Penelope Grace stood at the water's edge, a small smile on her face. "How beautiful," she whispered.

"Aye," Aira agreed. "But what lies beneath is altogether more wonderful."

Tilly trotted up. "I'm so glad we can agree on somethin', Aira," she said, her small teeth flashing as she let out a high-pitched yowl as if announcing their arrival.

Penelope waited with bated breath, but nothing happened at first. Then, the graceful birds began to turn in an ever-widening circle across the lake's icy surface. They reminded Penelope of clockwork animals as they drew closer and closer to the shore, leaving behind them a wide opening in the lake.

At last, one swan ceased its glide across the lake directly in front of their company. Just behind it, the surface of the lake had disappeared to reveal a set of stairs carved out of ice and stone. They reminded Penelope Grace of the creaky wooden stairs on the second floor of her home, not for their appearance, but for the way each drew you in, whispering to you of what might be found at stairway's end.

Tilly was the first to begin the descent, but Penelope was not far behind her. With each step, her already frosty breath became more visible as the temperature dropped; still, the cold here seemed to possess no power to numb or bite against Penelope's skin. She continued on, undeterred, her fingers tracing the carvings in the silver-grey wall.

You can imagine that, by the time she reached the bottom step, a young woman like Penelope Grace had already conjured up a thousand different possibilities for who this mysterious Ice Maiden might be. Yet, it is strange how, at times, the apparent wonder of imagining can seem utterly pale in comparison to reality.

Now, reader, I must ask you to close your eyes before we continue.

The Ice Maiden is an entirely unique being and not one to be imagined or passed over too quickly. Very little is known about the Ismeyjar, save that there is only ever one. They are beautiful, to be sure, yet you will find that that is never what is remembered about them. Their purpose is singular and experienced differently by all who share the delight of meeting them.

But first, a question.

Have you ever felt that hope is an ephemeral thing?

When circumstances aren't what you expected, have you ever tried to take hold of it, only to have it fall right through your fingers as if it had no substance, like a reflection in disturbed waters?

Yes, I know the feeling, too.

Still, hope is planted in each of us uniquely, though its source is always the same. The Ismeyjar have received the gift of reminding us what the substance of our hope is when we've forgotten.

Now, what I'm going to ask of you will be difficult if you have ever longed for hope and felt the sting of its loss. I want you to welcome some light into your dark places and let the Ismey remind you what hope looks like.

Are your eyes closed?

Good.

Deep breath now, friend, and take a step.

Penelope Grace stood frozen on the bottom step, hesitant to disturb the stillness of this stunning place. Her fingers grazed the cold stone banister that had been skillfully carved on either side of the last dozen steps.

The room waiting before her felt refreshing and crisp. Stone pillars lined the hall, and Penelope admired the carvings on the nearest of these. Delicate stone tendrils, like frozen ivy, climbed up the pillar, curving around intricate snowflakes. Real frost adorned these, causing them to shimmer as they caught the light.

But Penelope noticed that no torches adorned the walls; there was no discernible source of light at all, yet the room was filled with a fresh, radiant glow. She stepped into the room, at last, followed closely by Aira, who was looking with great joy at the figure just now appearing at the opposite end of the hall.

Penelope Grace's breath caught, and her companions grew quiet and still. She knew instantly that the figure was the Ice Maiden that everyone had been whispering about since their journey through the forest began.

The Ice Maiden's gown looked as if countless thousands of tiny snowflakes had swirled up in a great rush only to fall gracefully and weave together to form an icy covering that brushed softly against the stone floor as she walked towards them. Much like the pillars to either side, a thin layer of flakes and curving vines rose above the gown's neckline and down the Maiden's arms, catching the light and giving her ebony skin a steady radiance.

A look of such contentment warmed Penelope Grace's features as the Ice Maiden came to stand before her, and for just a moment, she could recall the way winter reminded her that no amount of fear or despair could outlast God's faithfulness and love, and the fear of what might be was banished by stillness and wonder.

The Ismey said nothing, but held out her hand, intending for Penelope to walk with her and enter the frozen stronghold. Penelope grasped her hand without question, and the entire company made their way down the hall. A soft breeze played across her skin as she walked, and a sudden dusting of snow swirled around her.

Penelope Grace closed her eyes, breathing in the invigorating cold, remembering brilliantly chilly nights just like this one when she had walked with her family through the snow. She would walk with them in the same way again, she knew, down a cobblestone street blanketed in white. And they would think of Uncle Alex and miss him terribly as they remembered the many nights that he had joined them, but still, they would walk, together and content because of it.

Penelope Grace looked over at the Ice Maiden, her heart impossibly full of gratitude for this precious gift, inexplicably given. She understood now why Elafry had refrained from telling her more about the Ice Maiden. The Ismeyjar were created to be givers of a gift that could not be expressed, only felt.

The Ice Maiden returned Penelope's look with a steady gaze, her eyes brilliant for the joy of seeing her gift flourishing for the good of others.

The moment passed, and Penelope found the stillness fading, replaced by a sudden warmth as they approached a massive set of carved wooden doors, opened just far enough that she could see the blazing roar of a large fire and hear the dull roar of conversation. Tilly trotted past her, letting out a joyous yip to announce their arrival.

The room was filled with several long, wooden tables lined with benches, and a large fireplace dominated the opposite wall. But it was not the room that made Penelope Grace look around in awe, but rather its inhabitants. There were dozens of arctic foxes pouncing on each other near the crackling fireplace, a quiet family of beavers, leopards, great bears, and many others that she supposed might be family to those who had greeted her at the winter carousel. Just as impossibly as the rest, they were all talking, a sight that Penelope Grace had never believed she would see.

These were the types of things that happened in storybooks, and she was still stunned by the sensation of suddenly living in one. She suspected, though, that this strange land was far from finished with surprising her. The Ismey and Aira guided her to comfortable seating by the fire, and Penelope observed the people in the room. There were what she believed to be satyrs, just as playful and boisterous as her books had led her to believe; elves, steadfast and graceful in all their movements; dwarves, steady and unyielding; and countless others.

Penelope forced herself to not rudely stare. She was only partially successful, for when she looked away from the tables, she noticed the great evergreen rising tall above her. Nothing adorned its branches, or so Penelope thought at first glance. But as she looked closer, she saw tiny glimmers of light peeking through the boughs.

Suddenly, one such light shot from a nearby branch, determinedly chasing another like it. Penelope heard a faint laugh as the two abandoned the tree and flickered quickly past her. She turned around, trying to catch sight of them again. Her efforts were rewarded when both lights stopped in front of her, Penelope Grace's curiosity matched by theirs.

She had to blink several times before she grew used to the light and could see the details of the tiny beings who were scrutinizing Penelope as they hovered in front of her. They were each clothed in warm pants and hooded coats, which were stitched with intricate detail. After a moment, they seemed to decide that Penelope would do and waved at her. Penelope was just returning the gesture when Tilly, displaying surprising, light-hearted mischief, jumped just beneath the fairies, yipping playfully as she allowed her jaws to snap closed just beneath their feet.

Both fairies let out startled shrieks and shot away, but recovering quickly, one of the delicate, winged creatures whipped around in the air and pointed at Tilly, sending out a quick burst of frost that was aimed directly at the fox's nose. Tilly let out a yelp as the sudden cold found its mark, swiping at her twitching nose to remove the snow.

Penelope laughed, Aira joining her. "You ought to know better by now, Tilly," the wolf teased.

But the fox offered a mischievous grin, saying, "It was worth it for the look on their wee faces," before wandering off between the tables to find food and a place to rest.

Penelope smiled before sinking into a cushy armchair by the fire. The Ismey took a seat opposite her, and Aira curled up on the floor between them. She felt that her words were frozen, though her mind tumbled with questions. Still, she had to speak, and since the figure across from her seemed content to wait, Penelope Grace took a deep breath and began. "You are the Ice Maiden," she ventured tentatively.

She received a smile in return. "Yes, I am the Ismey. Arabella is my name."

"I'm Penelope Grace," she answered, but the look on Arabella's face gave Penelope the distinct impression that she had, somehow, already known that.

The ice had been broken, but Penelope still had no idea where to start. Dozens of questions vied for attention, and she tried to sort through them for the most important, but it was ultimately the seemingly least important that escaped from her lips. "Why aren't my hands cold?"

Arabella laughed, her brown eyes sparkling with delight, before answering. "Only humans who carry Apricity may enter and travel safely through our land. Ellura is bitterly cold, and only the warmth of Apricity can sustain them. To my eyes, you burn brightly with it, and so you will be able to sense the cold, but it will not harm you."

Penelope nodded, but frowned. "Then… why can Denagon survive here? Or his allies, like the one who hunted us in the forest? Surely, they don't carry Apricity?"

"No, they do not. But neither Denagon nor his slaves are human."

She felt a deep chill at Arabella's words and turned her eyes away to look into the fire. 'Why am I here?" she whispered.

"To defend Apricity," Arabella answered. "Why you, in particular, were chosen, is not for me to say."

Penelope Grace shook her head, wrestling with confusion now that the initial awe of this stronghold was beginning to fade. "How is this place… possible?" she asked, her eyes meeting Arabella's.

"Our world was created with remarkable intention and care, just as yours was. Humans used to travel here of old, but the way was broken." Arabella paused. "Your grandmother helped to mend it."

At this, Penelope sat forward, eager to hear more of her grandmother's time in Ellura. It gave her comfort that she was not alone in having come here. "The carousel? How does it work?"

"There are Pathways between your world and others, Penelope. I do not claim to know the intricacies of how they work, but they make it possible to travel between worlds."

"And my grandmother? She mended a Pathway?"

Arabella hesitated before answering. "She did her part, Penelope."

"Did you know her?"

"No, I did not. But I know your grandmother's story because of this," she said, lightly touching the necklace she wore, which Penelope had not noticed until now.

The necklace bore a lovely pattern — silver leaves curving gracefully on either side of two brilliant gems, one pale blue and the other a deep navy. The firelight reflected off of these beautifully.

Arabella continued. "This necklace is a gift given to me by my sisters. There is only one Ismey at any given time, but we pass down our memories to each other through this," she said, her fingers tracing the delicate leaves. "I did not know your grandmother, Penelope Grace, but I do have the honor of carrying her story with me."

Tears welled in Penelope's eyes. "Tell me?"

"Before you leave," the Ice Maiden promised, "I will share it with you."

They sat quietly for several minutes, Penelope staring into the fire and Arabella watching the young woman and offering up a prayer that she would come to understand her place in this struggle against Denagon's destructive greed. It was not, in the end, up to Penelope to be strong enough, but it would take time yet for her to learn this, and still longer for her to find comfort in it.

Arabella could see more questions brewing in the girl's mind, but she rose and extended her hand to Penelope. "I know you have much left to ask, but for tonight, enjoy a good meal and rest."

Penelope Grace hesitated momentarily before taking the Ice Maiden's hand. She wanted so badly to uncover a solution that would make all things right, make her family well again, but there was a part of her that knew wisdom when she heard it. She took Arabella's hand and followed her through the maze of tables.

Yet, Denagon never left her mind, and the many unknowns of the coming days never left her thoughts. And though she found herself nestled in warm blankets late that evening, the memory of her family's frozen skin remained with her through the long night.

Penelope Grace woke to the soft sound of chimes. She opened her eyes, searching for the source of the noise, only to find several fairies hovering above her, speaking in their own tongue. Their voices were so small and melodic that Penelope's still sleep-filled mind had mistaken it for music.

Seeing that she was awake, the winged creatures burst into a fresh wave of conversation, now speaking words that she could have understood had they not all been talking at once. Finally, a fairy with pale lavender wings pushed her way to the front of the floating group, giving them all a stern look that managed to quiet the others.

"The Ismey is asking for you, my lady," the fairy announced, clearly pleased that she had been the one to deliver the Ice Maiden's message. The others huffed but flitted off after the lucky messenger once Penelope began to rise.

Her room was spare but warm. The furniture was simple, carefully carved from wood, but unadorned. There was a simple bed frame, a chair, and a table with a candle still flickering atop it. On the other side of the bed was a small hearth that somehow warmed the room without producing smoke. But all of these things only raised more questions for Penelope Grace. How was it possible to have smokeless flames? And how did they ever manage to bring furniture into a stronghold so deep underground? Though Penelope firmly believed that not all mysteries are meant to be understood, she hoped that some of her questions would be answered.

Penelope noticed that on the chair lay a set of more practical clothes: soft pants that looked thin but were surprisingly warm, a fitted, long-sleeved shirt, a hooded coat, lined with unfamiliar, insulating material, and lastly, a pair of laced boots. She dressed quickly, but found herself unable, at first, to adjust to the strange apparel, so different from what she usually wore.

Her room was not far from the main hall, and she found her way there quickly. Aira, waiting by the entrance, rose at Penelope's arrival, and together, they navigated a series of tunnels. They had traveled some distance when Penelope heard the resounding rush of water. Curious, she peered into a deep cavern, which seemed to be the source of the noise, her eyes widening as she did. A small lake nearly filled the entire cavern, fed by a river that rushed into the stronghold from above. A great many dwarves stood to either side of the lake, using long poles to guide thick logs to the water's shore.

Well, that answered at least one of her questions. They did not bring furniture into the stronghold at all, only the means by which to fashion it. Feeling a measure of satisfaction, Penelope continued following Aira. Shortly after, they reached their destination. The room was small, dominated by a large table with a map that was secured to the corners.

The Ismey waited for them, her demeanor much more serious than the previous night. "You slept well, Penelope Grace?"

"Well enough, thank you," Penelope replied, then stepped forward to look more closely at the map.

One could tell at a glance that it was hand drawn with incredible skill and attention to detail. Penelope's eyes searched carefully to see if she could spot anything familiar and quickly found a miniature reproduction of the carousel nestled in the middle of a vast forest. Penelope then found the river and followed it to the lake and sculpted swans – the entrance to this hidden fortress.

Staring at the map, she understood now just how sweeping Ellura was, and she felt unsteady at the thought that she was indeed in an entirely different world. But then her eyes caught movement across the paper. Penelope's gaze wandered to the far end of the map, and she noticed a creeping darkness like someone had only just spilled a well of ink that was masking the intricate craftsmanship of the land.

She looked up in alarm at Arabella, who watched her with a steady, solemn gaze. "The map not only shows one the way through Ellura but also reveals the state of the land. Some months ago, our people fought against Denagon and his creatures, but he defeated us and overpowered my home, Leitad. The shadow that accompanies him continues to spread across the land, and my home has since become known as Svarthol."

Penelope's heart ached to see her own loss mirrored in Arabella's and Aira's eyes. She was separated from her family because of Denagon's attacks, it was true, but everyone gathered here had lost family, friends, and their homes. They had risked their lives to defend an entire land from this evil, and they had not stopped there.

Recognizing that Denagon's evil was not confined to Ellura, Aira had crossed from one world to the next, all for the sake of a young woman who was frightened and alone. True, it seemed that Penelope's gift of Apricity was somehow vital to overcoming Denagon. Still, the inhabitants of Ellura could have closed their borders and turned away as Penelope's world fell to the darkness, complacent in the knowledge that at least their land was secure. But they had not, and she was humbled by the generosity of their hearts.

"What can we do to stop this, Arabella?" Penelope asked, her eyes sparkling with determination.

"We must rekindle light where he has sown darkness. Doing so will drive him out. Denagon hates and fears nothing more than the Light. Because you were given Apricity, you are called to do your part."

"How?"

"You must make your way to Svarthol — not alone, for I will choose a small number of faithful companions to join you — and find your way into the fortress. Beyond that, I cannot say. Darkness such as this has never taken root in our land, and combatting something of this strength is foreign to us."

Penelope nodded, refusing to be daunted by the Ice Maiden's words. It seemed an impossible task, but at this moment in time, Penelope Grace felt the urgency of Ellura's plight, and she had witnessed for herself what Denagon's evil could do. If she could prevent more suffering, she would do her part. She met Arabella's gaze. "When do we leave?"

"If you are still willing, tonight," the Ismey replied.

With this decided, the three of them left the room. Arabella disappeared to an unknown part of the stronghold, while Penelope and Aira returned to the hall, where the wolf insisted that she eat. "You will need all your strength in the coming days, Penelope," Aira said as a steaming plate of food was placed before her.

"Will you be coming with me?" she asked hopefully.

Aira returned her question with a fierce look. "No matter the dangers that threaten us, I will not leave your side."

Penelope Grace smiled, warmed by the wolf's response, and relieved that she would have Aira's protection and companionship on the journey.

Throughout the rest of the day, provisions were gathered and packed, and it was decided that Tilly, Wynnfelde – along with her cubs, Frederick and Eloise, for she would not leave them – as well as Copernicus and Elafry would join Penelope and Aira on the long trek to Svarthol. As evening fell, they made ready to leave, and Penelope felt a twinge of sadness and trepidation at the thought of forsaking the safety of the underground fortress. She knew, though, that time was not something to be wasted if they hoped to defend people against Denagon and the coming darkness.

With that thought in mind, the small company ventured out into the cold, starlit night.

The messenger crept into the room, unwilling to deliver his news now that he must face his master. His claws scrabbled against the floor, searching for purchase against the unforgiving ice. Deep shadow dominated the far corner, shaking with every ragged breath.

Again, the messenger hesitated. Two nights ago, the master had returned, having suffered injury from the hated Light. The winged creature hissed softly at the thought, which inadvertently alerted the master to his presence.

Denagon rose, and the pale eyes locked on the suddenly servile creature. He said nothing; he did not need to. His eyes demanded an answer, one that his servant now rushed to give.

"Master, the girl… the one who serves the wicked Light." The shadow deepened at the mention of the wretch, but the servant continued, his voice a terrified whisper. "She has been seen. She is here, Master, in Ellura."

Denagon seemed to swell with sudden rage, and as the servant cowered, trying to slink away from the master's terrible anger, Denagon discovered that he still possessed enough strength to inflict pain. As he summoned two servants to drag the limp body away, Denagon felt reassured.

The darkness would always prove more potent than the Light, in the end. And if he could snuff out the life of a creature born of that darkness, a weakling girl would not prove too difficult a challenge.

Deep shadows gathered around his pale, drawn frame, and Denagon looked out on Svarthol with twisted anticipation.

She would come for him, he was sure.

But by the time she reached him, Denagon would see to it that the girl was terribly alone.

It would take them near a week to reach Svarthol, and Penelope felt her nerves grating against each other when she thought of all that time. She wondered how many of their neighbors and friends had also fallen prey to the wasting freeze, and she burned with anger at the way Denagon had perverted the beauty of winter into something that could only be understood as unforgiving and brutal.

There is a harshness to winter, it is true, but there is also a stillness that prepares the way for new life. To acknowledge one and reject the other is to rob winter of all its fullness and remarkable grace.

Yet, hearts often grow dismayed during the long stretches of winter nights; Penelope Grace watched it happen to those she loved and had fought against the sharpness of despair herself. She felt a growing desire to defend, not only the beauty of winter itself but also the hearts of all who struggled to find joy during this time of year. She wanted to fight against Denagon's attacks and keep him from succeeding in his destructive work.

Uncle Alex had said she was created to weave joy and delight — wonder — into people's lives, and now, when so many lives were at risk of freezing straight through, could she do any less than what he said? No matter how impossible, she must try, and with this thought fueling her, Penelope Grace walked purposefully through Ellura, hardly seeing the beauty of the world around her through the first day of travel.

Aira watched her closely. She feared what determination might do to the girl, for she had seen for herself the way that a desire to save could undo a human. But she held her tongue for the moment, watching still, but patiently.

On the second day of their journey, she separated from the company, believing that a particular grove was nearby and that such a place might spark something different in Penelope's heart. By evening the wolf returned, her supposition proven right. As the sky darkened and countless stars winked into sight, Aira and Penelope left the campsite and wound their way through the forest.

"Aira, where are we going?" Penelope asked, wanting only to rest after two days of unfamiliar exertion.

"Hush, child," the wolf replied, her tone kind but firm. "You'll scare them off."

Penelope Grace tried her best to remain silent from that point on, but the snowy ground had turned to hoar frost beneath her feet, and each footfall betrayed her with a loud crunch. Despite her own difficulties, Aira somehow had no trouble walking silently through the snow, and Penelope thought to herself how grateful she was that the wolf was not her enemy.

After some time, they came to the edge of a small grove, one that Penelope would have certainly missed for the trees were quite close together in this part of the forest. Carefully now, she tiptoed to the edge of the grove and peered beyond the branches, hurrying to stifle an awestruck gasp as she did so.

The plants, grass, and trees themselves – every inch of this wintry grove – were all covered in beautifully crisp frost. This sanctuary in the heart of the forest was cloaked in blue light, though Penelope Grace could not find its source; it seemed to emanate softly from everything and everyone present as if they were reflecting the light of a silver-blue sun.

At first, she could not discern details, but soon Penelope noticed beautiful small figures gliding through the air.

She thought that frost fairies populated the grove, but when she leaned down to quietly ask Aira, the wolf corrected her. "Snow sprites. Similar in nature, but with a beauty quite their own. Now, look."

Penelope edged as close as she dared to the smallest of gaps in the trees where she might see the snow sprites more closely. To her delight, several were beginning to swirl through the snow as they circled the grove, and they flew quite close.

Each snow sprite wore beautiful, deep blue gowns, etched with frost and shimmering with the clearing's light. Their hair was silvery-white, and their skin a pale blue. There seemed to be hundreds of them, and as they all flew about the grove, they began to hum the most enchanting tune.

You can almost hear it, can't you? Like the melody from a favorite music box that you can't quite remember, but nevertheless, remains with you.

Penelope listened, not daring to make a sound.

The snow sprites slowly gathered around a frozen pool in the center of the grove. The sound of their melody stayed soft as each took their turn in gliding across the pool's frozen surface, leaving behind a precise etching in the ice. As every snow sprite made their simple contribution, they left the grove behind them, and they continued in this way until the frost-covered sanctuary stood empty.

Penelope looked questioningly at Aira, and the wolf gave her a slight nod, indicating it was safe now to enter the grove. She stepped carefully through the small gap and approached the pool, gasping to see the impossibly intricate snowflake traced into its icy surface.

"Their winter dance is a yearly tradition of the snow sprites. They travel from all across Ellura to make their contribution to the snowflake."

"It's beautiful, Aira. But why do they do it?" Penelope asked.

The wolf looked up at her intently before answering. "It is a celebration to honor the One who made them, to rejoice in the delight and wonder of being created."

Aira fell silent, but then met Penelope's gaze earnestly. "You see, Penelope Grace, it is not so much that you are living in wonder. It is Who you are living in wonder of."

At this, the wolf turned, and Penelope Grace followed, feeling once again the conviction that she had just heard words that were worthy of remembering.

Aira woke Penelope with an urgent nudge to her forearm. "Penelope," the wolf whispered. "We must run."

She was up in a heartbeat, not fully understanding the gravity of the danger in her tired state. Stumbling through the forest after her companions, Penelope Grace struggled to remain steady on the uneven ground.

Elafry ran up and remained close beside her, glancing worriedly at the exhausted girl. When she stumbled over a snow-covered log and landed roughly on her knees, the lion quickly lay on the ground beside her. As the snow blew around them, Penelope struggled to distinguish between the swirling storm and Elafry's white coat.

"Climb on my back, Penelope Grace. I will carry you."

She shook her head, wincing at the pain in her ankle. "I will only slow you."

Elafry let out an impatient growl. "We cannot afford to argue. Now climb on my back!"

Penelope knew he was right. She did not understand what they were fleeing from, but she knew time was not something they had an abundance of.

Quickly, she climbed onto the lion's back, stumbling awkwardly when she tried to put weight on her left foot. She managed it swiftly enough, though, and Elafry flew, racing through the trees, his claws digging powerfully into the frozen earth with every determined stride.

In the early dawn, when the light reflecting off of snow is only a dim, haunting blue, Penelope Grace struggled to make out the shapes of her friends, let alone the enemy hunting them. But soon enough, Wynnfelde's imposing form appeared, stark against the tall trees and the rushing river only feet behind her.

A hideous creature stalked her. Its skin had a rough, leathery appearance, yet it was paper-thin, and Penelope could clearly see the creature's bones, shifting with each movement. It spread its enormous wings, letting out a horrible shriek that chilled Penelope Grace and her companions.

But Wynnfelde would not be shaken. Her cubs — young Frederick and Eloise — stood just behind her, but had equally fierce expressions on their faces that dared the beast to charge them.

The beast dared.

With a furious, triumphant scream, it bounded through the snow, the claws on the end of its mighty wings giving it traction as it used them to surge forward. Wynnfelde prepared herself, bellowing a challenge, but she misunderstood the creature's intent. Just seconds before it would have collided with the fearsome polar bear, the creature dodged to the right, tackling Eloise.

The cub fought, wrestling to escape, but she was hopelessly tangled in the confusion of great wings and sharp claws, and with a triumphant shove from the creature and a fearful cry from the cub, Eloise tumbled into the rapid river.

Before Wynnfelde could take a breath, Frederick leaped in after her, but he was soon swept up in the river's current and, for all his courage and devotion, was unable to help his sister. Wynnfelde let out the desperate, keening cry of a mother separated from her children — something that is really more felt than heard — and raced down the riverbank, heedless of the creature now that her cubs were in such danger. Copernicus leapt after her, knowing she could not hope to rescue them alone.

Only Aira, Elafry, and Tilly remained to face the winged beast. But as they readied themselves for the battle, dread crept over them. Out of the trees emerged several more creatures, some winged like their first attacker, some tall and broad, terribly confident in their strength. They were outnumbered and tiring. Penelope's mind raced, wondering what they would do. But then Elafry did something entirely unexpected.

Foes on every side, every way out seemingly impassable, but Elafry knelt down in the snow.

Penelope's heart beat wildly. What was he doing? She leaned down quietly and saw that his eyes were closed, but still, she dared to urgently whisper his name. "Elafry?"

He did not answer. But a moment later, he rose, and his strength and determination seemed renewed.

Penelope and her companions stood utterly still, waiting for their enemies to make a move.

They already had.

With a piercing shriek, one of the winged creatures leapt from a high branch, digging its claws into Elafry's back, nearly raking Penelope's shoulder as it landed. The lion roared in pain, stumbling as he fought to loosen the beast's hold. Penelope Grace only allowed herself to think for a moment before she tumbled from Elafry's back, knowing she was hindering him.

She looked around, desperately searching for some kind of weapon, but found nothing. Elafry continued to struggle, unable to either remove or fight the creature clinging to him. Seconds later, Aira took several bounds past her. Penelope shuddered at the horrible ripping sound as Aira's claws shredded the creature's wings, simultaneously tearing him loose from the lion's back.

Elafry did not let his wounds slow him. As Aira dashed out of reach, Elafry rounded on the now whimpering creature, his powerful muscles bunching as he moved. The beast hissed as the lion bore down on it, but any attempt it might have made to fight was cut short, and its body soon lay limp in the snow.

Penelope Grace felt lost in the fray. All around her, friends and enemies alike were fighting. She had no weapon, and she was doing nothing to help. Brushing frustrated tears from her face, Penelope rose, determined to do something.

Tilly!

Where was the little fox? Penelope wondered with a start.

In moments, she heard Tilly, the taunts of the bold fox somehow managing to rise above the battle. Refusing to be undone by the pain in her ankle, Penelope followed the fox's voice, hoping to find a weapon on the way, for she knew that Tilly would need help against foes so much bigger than she.

She was almost to the fox when Penelope felt a searing line of heat slice down her left arm. Stunned by the pain, she dropped to one knee in the snow, breathing heavily and trying to get her bearings. Above her, a thick-limbed beast leered down, clearly anticipating an easy kill.

Penelope could not move. Her breath came in ragged gasps, and her vision began to fog over from the pain.

He raised the ugly blade that had wounded her once already.

But just as he made to strike, the beast's face twisted in a pained grimace, and he let out a desperate, furious howl as he fell.

Unbeknownst to Penelope or her attacker, Tilly had wound her way through the chaos to the young woman's aid, and her teeth were now firmly sunk into the tendon of the beast's ankle. Before the creature could recover, Aira was on top of him, her jaws around his throat for only a second before he was no longer a threat.

Aira rushed to Penelope, whose head still hung from the shock of the pain. "Penelope Grace, you must get up."

She raised her head just enough to look the wolf in the eye. Letting out an impatient grunt, Aira came around behind Penelope and shoved her muzzle beneath the girl's right arm, helping her to rise.

Looking at the fox, Aira spoke quickly. "Tilly, tear off a piece of her cloak."

Aira's attention returned to Penelope. "Bind your arm tightly now. We have very little time."

Her fingers felt clumsy from the pain, but Penelope Grace managed to do as Aira said. Exhausted, she leaned against Aira's side gratefully, but just then, Elafry let out a ragged roar.

Penelope Grace looked around in alarm, letting out a horrified gasp when she saw that the white lion was swarmed by Denagon's servants. With terrifying persistence, the creatures had taken advantage of Aira's distraction and borne Elafry to the ground through sheer numbers. Aira bolted from Penelope and Tilly without a word, a howl of challenge echoing through the forest as she did.

"We have to help them!" Penelope cried.

"No!" Tilly barked. "Ye must run with me."

"I can't run –," Penelope argued, indignant, but the fox's eyes flashed in anger, and it was enough to silence her.

"D'ye not see? Denagon will do anythin' to keep ye from reachin' Svarthol. At all costs, we must keep ye safe."

She knew that Tilly was right; still, it grated against every nerve in her body to leave her friends behind. But if they did not reach Svarthol, if they did not try to rekindle light, Denagon's hold over Ellura would be irrevocable. Her own world would fall alongside Ellura, and her family would be lost, forgotten in a land of eternal darkness and ice.

They ran through the forest, praying that Aira and Elafry would be enough of a distraction to keep the creatures from noticing their absence.

They almost made it.

But one of the winged creatures was particularly cunning, and his eyes overlooked nothing. He had remained in the treetops, expecting a desperate attempt to escape just like this one. The creature waited several seconds, allowing the girl and the whelp a few moments to believe themselves free, and then he rose from the trees and followed swiftly behind.

When he was perhaps a dozen feet behind the pair, he let his claws rake against the treetops, causing a startling noise that brought the fox up short. The girl, in her panic, kept running. It was several seconds before she realized the fox was not with her, and by then, it was too late.

The winged creature landed just behind the girl, relishing the look of sheer panic as it settled in her bones that she was cut off from her only remaining friend. She stumbled back, clutching her bleeding arm as she scrambled for some way of fighting him.

His eyes were lit with malicious glee.

A jolt of panic shocked Penelope as she realized that Tilly was nowhere in sight. But the beast was still bearing down on her, and she still had no weapon with which to fight him. Then, with a sudden yowl and a bright flash of fur, Tilly leapt from a thick branch onto the beast's head. He let out a horrible scream of rage and pain, while Tilly clawed at his eyes, knowing they must incapacitate a creature that they could not match in strength.

Blood trickled down his cheeks, but it was only a moment later that he managed to tear Tilly loose, and the fox landed with a loud yelp on the snow-covered ground and was still.

But Penelope had not been idle. Just as the beast wrenched Tilly's claws from his face, Penelope Grace threw a large, well-aimed rock at his bloodied head, and with a loud thump, their attacker crumpled to the ground.

She whirled round to help Tilly, to protect her if she could, and stopped short as her stomach dropped like a stone. All Penelope saw was a pale face and flat, black eyes staring out at her from a ragged, wisp-thin cloak, grey against the snow-laden trees.

Stumbling backward, Penelope tried to look away and could not. The figure floated just above the frozen ground, free from the dangers of rocks or limbs that were disguised by the snow. It came towards her slowly, relishing her inability to escape or run.

A pale hand extended towards Penelope and seemed to hold her in place. She continued to try to back away, but her movements felt slow, as though she were waist-deep in water, and the figure was closer now, its black eyes bearing down on her.

Penelope cried out in sudden pain.

A sharp, unrelenting bite dug into her heel, jerking her free from the figure's gaze. Just in time, Penelope Grace darted out of reach.

She had escaped whatever fate had awaited her, but the strange creature now rounded on her protector, furious that its attack had been foiled. Tilly was quick, but the pale figure's rage lent it speed, and its claws shot out at the little fox.

"Run, girl!" Tilly shouted, and then she was lost to Penelope's view.

Chaos raged around her, and she stood, unnoticed for a brief time, in the midst of it. She could hear Elafry's fierce roars tearing through the night air, but it sounded to her that he was suffering pain rather than inflicting it. Though Penelope searched, she could find no sign of Aira, and Tilly was lost to her.

She had to get out.

She had to run.

Praying that none of Denagon's many servants caught sight of her, Penelope Grace bolted through the forest, desperately searching for a place to hide. But her thoughts were so scattered, how could she find a place in time?

She ran past a massive oak and felt an intense pull to go back. Circling it quickly, Penelope found that at its base, there was an opening, just large enough for her to fit. With no time to question its safety, she crawled inside and found that the tree disguised a surprisingly large hollow.

Penelope Grace moved to the far wall and curled up in a tight ball. She could not stop the relentless shaking of her hands or of her shoulders as she cried, choking back any sound for fear that it would give her hiding place away.

This was too much like home, too much like watching, helpless, as Denagon tore her family away from her.

It felt like a terribly long time before Penelope fell into a fitful sleep.

She woke to find two bright, brown eyes looking down at her. "Tilly!" Penelope cried, impossibly happy to find her friend returned to her.

The fox turned in a quick circle, equally pleased to have found the girl safe and sound.

"How did you find me? Are Elafry and Aira with you?"

"Yer tracks helped a bit," Tilly said before nudging Penelope's arm to soften her chiding.

Penelope's eyes widened. She was horrified by the thought that any of those wicked creatures could have found her were it not for her faithful friend.

Tilly, seeing her embarrassment, said, "Never ye mind about it now, girl. But should we be separated again, be sure to cover them. Ye never know when someone less friendly may be followin' ye."

"Thank you, Tilly," Penelope replied, resisting the urge to give the fox a rewarding scratch behind her ear. She suspected Tilly would not welcome being treated like an adorable animal, true though it may be. "And the others?"

At this, Tilly shook her head, her disappointment evident. "Aira was separated from us. I canna say where she might be. Not long after ye left, Denagon's creatures began to scatter suddenly, retreatin' through the forest to wreak havoc elsewhere."

The fox's expression grew grim. "The elsewhere is what worries us. Elafry found me after the battle, and we decided it best for him to warn those he could. He'll outrun the creatures, I'm certain. Whether there'll be time enough for anyone to flee is a differen' matter."

"Well, we have to help them!" Penelope insisted.

"No," Tilly replied, surprising Penelope with her firm tone. "Ye must reach Svarthol and do jus' what the Ismey said. That will be challenge enough with yer injuries, and all the bravery in the world willna' save them if ye don't do what ye were brought here for."

She wanted to argue, but Tilly was right. Light restored was what Ellura and its people most needed, and if she could do this one thing, perhaps all would be well for them and her family once more.

"Do you think it is safe to leave now?"

Tilly shook her head. "No. We wait for mornin'. His creatures willna' be so active in the daylight."

They settled down to wait. But something nagged at Penelope Grace's mind. "Tilly," she asked, "why did Elafry kneel before the battle began?"

One brown eye opened. "He was prayin'."

Struck by her answer, Penelope fell silent.

The fox urged her to rest, but she could not. She wondered what was waiting for them at Denagon's fortress, and feared her ability to overcome it. How could she find the strength to overcome such darkness?

How, indeed, reader?

How indeed?

As the sixth day dawned, marking a week since they had left the underground fortress, Penelope and Tilly arrived at the end of the forest. Her injuries had slowed them somewhat, but the fox had kept a careful eye on her and instructed Penelope in the use of herbs that helped her arm to safely heal. Below them stretched a dark, endless valley that no sunlight seemed to reach.

Nothing grew there. The valley was stunted and barren, its flat expanse only broken by the twisted stronghold that rose up in its center like a scar on the land. Its towers, made of black, implacable rock, rose up. Ice smothered every surface, and in this view, Penelope Grace could see what people feared in her favorite season.

Svarthol was the long, dreaded march of endless winter, without the promise of new life to come. Tilly interrupted her thoughts. "Are ye ready, Penelope Grace?"

"Yes," she whispered, taking a deep breath as she continued to gaze down into the valley. "I don't suppose daylight will be too helpful to us in there."

"Aye. But ye have Light of an altogether differen' sort to guide ye. Let's be off," Tilly concluded, not explaining her words as she trotted down the only rutted path to Svarthol.

Once they entered the valley, Penelope Grace was horribly on edge, though there were none of the dangers she had anticipated. None of Denagon's creatures lurked behind the dry husks of once tall trees. Nothing stalked them or sought to prevent their progress on the long stretch to Svarthol's entrance.

The valley was desolate and still, and Penelope was all the more terrified because of it.

Something was not right.

A vast expanse of land separated them from Svarthol's gates when Penelope Grace stopped short and whirled around, knowing that she had heard the whisper of something behind her.

"Tilly..."

The fox saw it and barked a warning that was drowned out by the roar of bursting earth and the dull murmur of creeping vines.

They were separated before a thing could be done.

Nearly choking on the dusty earth clouding the air, Penelope cried out, "Tilly!"

No answer.

"*Tilly!*"

She spun about, peering through the dust-choked air for some sign of her friend. Reaching forward to keep herself steady, Penelope's finger scraped against something sharp, and she jerked back in pain.

She stood still, breathing hard, listening, and waiting.

But when the dust at last cleared, Penelope Grace was alone, just as she had feared, shut in by a twisting maze of bracken and thorns.

Penelope Grace thought she might break for the weight of this final barrier, isolating her from her last remaining friend. The twisting, tangled walls of the maze rose high above her, blocking out what little light had managed to filter through the dense clouds. She stood, frozen, for several tense seconds, not knowing what to do or which way to go.

Peering up ahead, Penelope could see the sharp turns of the maze, and she shivered at the thought of never knowing what might be waiting for her just out of sight.

Nevertheless, she had to make a choice. Right or left?

Which would you choose, reader, if I may ask?

Left?

If you say so.

Left Penelope Grace went, but she only managed three more turns through the maze before she was brought up short by a dead end.

Her heartbeat picked up.

Back she went, but when she came to the second turn, she noticed a new path, and rather than go back to the start, Penelope Grace turned right.

Several more turns. Another dead end.

But this time, just as she turned around, Penelope Grace noticed a warm glow emanating from the path she had just taken. Retracing her steps eagerly, she stopped short beneath the unexpected source of light.

An intricately twisted piece of metal now emerged from the cloying bracken of the maze, and from it hung an old, iron lantern, which housed the light within. Penelope watched in fascination as the tendrils of bracken crept along the cold metal, determined to overtake it, but shrunk away as soon as they came too near the lantern's light. Peering closer, Penelope could not see what the light's source was, but more than that, she was positive that this lantern had not been there only minutes before.

She could not afford to stand here and puzzle out its meaning, though. Only one more turn remained before she reached her last starting point, and inviting as the light's warmth might be, she had to continue on her way.

She would find her way out of this maze, Penelope thought, and with that determination, she found her next turn, never noticing the lantern hanging above her path, empty of light.

Penelope Grace could not have told you how long she wandered in the maze when total darkness fell, and nor can I.

All I can say now is that she is thoroughly lost in the heart of it, and it remains to be seen by what means she will find a way out.

Frantically, she raced from one dead end to another, certain at times that she had, at last, found the right path, and equally certain at other times that any hope of finding a way out on her own was impossible.

On that count, at least, she was correct.

She came to a crossroads within the maze. Three untried (she hoped) paths were before her. One of those unusual lanterns hung at the start of each; only one of them was illuminated. Penelope Grace paused, considering which was her best option but only grew more indecisive by the moment.

A rustle behind her brought her sharply around, but she could see nothing through the gloomy haze. Sure she had not heard wrong, Penelope stared determinedly through the darkness for several tense seconds, before finally resigning herself to the uncomfortable fact that her fears were beginning to play tricks on her.

She turned back to the paths, all still awaiting her decision.

Squaring her shoulders, Penelope strode down the center path, leaving indecision behind her, along with the only lantern offering light to the maze for some distance.

Penelope, of course, was too set on her choice to hear the shifting of close-knit vines as the way back was firmly shut.

She had only decided on two more paths when another rustle sounded behind her. Penelope stopped short, but would not look back, would not let her fear get the best of her.

One deep breath and she moved forward again, fighting to remain sure of herself. This time something moved just to her right, not touching her, though she could feel the breath of it passing by.

Another rush of movement to her left. Penelope jumped back as she glanced frantically around for its source. Her cloak ripped as it caught on a thorn. Quickly now, Penelope Grace bent to untangle it from the bracken, her fingers clumsy.

The rustling sound grew louder, and as her cloak only grew more entangled, Penelope let out a cry of frustration and panic. Looking around for any kind of help, though she didn't know what she expected to find, Penelope froze.

A mass of thorns and brittle vines were unassumingly gathering in front of her, barring her way forward while she remained none the wiser.

Frightened and enraged, she ran forward, at last succeeding in wrenching her cloak free. But the way was shut before Penelope could reach it, and she stopped just short of beating against the solid wall of bracken, knowing that would only leave her hands a bloody, aching mess.

Penelope's mind raced, but there were countless paths through this maze. Surely, she could retrace her steps and find another.

Racing down the path, Penelope nearly stumbled over the enormous husk of a root that she knew had not been there before. Undeterred, she ran on. Though the mist was growing thicker, she could see the light from the lantern that had illuminated the crossroads and knew she was close.

She was almost on top of the barred path before she realized her mistake.

She could not go back.

Neither could she go forward.

How many more paths would the bracken prevent her from reaching? How long before every way was shut?

There was no way out.

She cried out in sudden pain. Looking down, she saw a thorn retreating from her. The whisper of the bracken's movement grew louder as Penelope stared down at her hand, where a thin, slow trickle of blood stood out starkly against her pale skin.

But it was not the pain of the scratch that caused her to cry out; it was the sharp sensation of the cold, something she had not felt since arriving in Ellura. Something Arabella had told her Apricity would shield her from.

What was happening?

Had she lost it? Penelope wondered in a panic, and the question was echoed in the triumphant rustle of bracken and vine.

It was only seconds before the maze surged forward to claim her.

Her vision felt clouded as she ran. Whether that was from the rising mist or her own fear, Penelope did not know. She gave no thought to which paths she took. The one thought driving her was escape from the teeming vines, but her legs were weak beneath her, and her skin was numbing from the deep chill.

She had to escape.

Her breath came in panicked gasps.

Seeing an opening immediately to her right, Penelope forced her legs to take the sharp turn, but they could no longer support the strain.

Her knees gave way, and Penelope crumpled to the hard ground. She looked up and saw that the path ahead, which grew steadily wider, remained open much to her surprise and hope. She could just make out what seemed like a clearing.

Could it be the way out?

Read on.

With a pained grunt, Penelope pushed herself up onto her knees. If she could just get up, she could make it.

The vine snaked up her leg before her hope could gain any traction. She made the mistake of struggling and cried out as the thorns dug deeper into her skin. The maze was closing in. Penelope had no weapon, nothing sharp to cut away at the bracken. Penelope Grace looked desperately around, but there was nothing left for her to do or try.

Yet, just as she had the thought, another, altogether different realization occurred to her. Through the loss of Uncle Alex, through every frightening moment when she thought the silence might engulf her, not once had she been left alone.

When grief and despair had kept her parents, Nurse Sasha, and Georgie from coming up for air, when her own vision for wonder was clouding, He had never failed to remain with her.

Faithful and steadfast, He had shown her a way out from danger, had reminded her why she could still dare to hope in the face of debilitating circumstances.

Having gone to such great lengths to help her see when she doubted and reveal the depths of His love, He certainly would not leave her now, and the fierceness of Penelope Grace's belief grew and grew.

The vines on her leg crumbled to dust as if the strain of their attack had finally taxed the last shred of life remaining to them.

Penelope did not wait to see what happened. Limping though she was, she hurried to the opening, which was illuminated on either side by two lanterns, their lights blazing brilliantly.

The area she entered was indeed a clearing, and she wondered if it might be the middle of the maze. Before Penelope stood a row of various paths, all of them open to her through a simple arch. All save one.

In the center was a door. Above it hung a solitary lantern, the only one of many scattered throughout the clearing that was lit.

With the simple realization, Penelope Grace understood.

The light.

With every wrong turn, every faltering step, He had been trying to lead her through the maze the whole time.

Each twisted piece of bracken and every vine seethed around her, breaking into Penelope's thoughts and reminding her of the urgency to be free of them. She ran for the door, unwavering in her choice to follow the path He laid out for her now.

She pressed down on the handle eagerly.

It was locked.

Penelope Grace dismissed the panic threatening her once again, confident that she would not have been led to the door for no reason. Perhaps, there was a key. She looked up at the vines around the door, which were always reaching for and retreating from the light, but she could see nothing in the entangled mess.

She looked around the clearing slowly, but there was nothing but empty space, the path back, and the way forward.

Knock.

The suddenness of the voice startled her, yet she was not afraid. Penelope searched the clearing once more, but there was no one else there, no other way of explaining the inexplicable, but clearly heard, voice.

There was nothing left to do but listen.

Softly now, Penelope knocked.

The door was opened, though she never touched the handle.

Pushing it further, Penelope Grace peered around to the other side and smiled. She was not yet at the end of the maze, but the mist had thinned, and she could see a lantern's brilliant light at the end of the path.

She raced towards it, unspeakably thankful that He had given her an answer to the maze's riddle long before she had the humility to ask.

Penelope arrived at the end of the maze more quickly than she anticipated. A low arch of rustling bracken, its thorns sharp as ever, served as the exit, but Penelope Grace passed beneath it without hesitation.

Fear of the maze could not paralyze her any longer. Terror was now replaced by blazing awe of the One who was both powerful and loving enough to lead her through it.

As she gazed up at Svarthol, towering above her, and considered the certainty that Denagon was waiting for her inside, Penelope Grace still hoped.

The weight of darkness smothering this once beautiful place was immense, and the task of lifting it was impossible by any logical standard.

And yet, despite all this, Penelope Grace could still walk towards the gates with her head held high in defiant faith.

She remembered the way He had lit up every dark place before now, and Denagon's stronghold would not prove more powerful than His faithfulness.

PART THREE: APRICITY

An unnatural wind blew fiercely around her slight frame, trying to dissuade her from her path, but Penelope Grace refused to turn back. Though she had to raise her soft velvet hood to shield her face against the stinging snow, she knew that Svarthol's gates were only a few dozen steps away; this last, desperate attempt on Denagon's part to keep her from entering would fail.

Still, the wind was relentlessly gusting all around her, driving the snow into immense drifts to either side, making even this short distance anything but simple to cross.

Imagine that you, reader, are sheltered beneath a velvet cloak, hunched over from the blistering wind. Peering through what seems a wall of snow, only blurry images can be made out before you must look down again.

You can understand, then, how a well-loved friend, nearly returned to Penelope, recognized the danger, but tugged at the hem of her cloak a fraction of a second too late.

Tilly yipped a sharp warning, but it was lost in a gust of wind.

As Penelope Grace stepped beneath the arch and pushed the gate open, a creak from rusting hinges filled the air, nearly disguising the soft growl coming from behind her. She turned, dreading whatever new danger awaited, and found two wolves with hackles raised.

Penelope gasped when she saw them, not for fear of what they might do, but for the shock of seeing that their bodies were formed entirely from rough stone.

She knew they must be Denagon's servants, though she wondered if that were by choice or force. Every inch of their carved frames made their ability to harm her clear, but Penelope's attention was drawn to their eyes. Even as these creatures bared their fangs and began to advance, their eyes held something more than the hatred she had encountered in Denagon's other slaves: a plea and real despair. The longer she looked, the less convinced she was that the wolves truly desired to harm her.

Knowing this was possibly her most foolhardy choice since arriving in Ellura, Penelope Grace reached out a hand to the nearest wolf, hoping against hope that she might cool his anger with a friendly touch.

Her fingers were nearly brushing against his muzzle when he lunged at her, jaws snapping. She jumped back with a yelp, while both wolves came closer, knowing she was trapped.

"This way, lass!" she heard a familiar voice shout.

There was no time to question the little fox's appearance or how she had snuck past the wolves. She was here and had found a way for Penelope to escape the jaws of Denagon's sentinels.

Just as both wolves lunged forward, Penelope Grace darted out of reach, and together, she and Tilly ran for the twisting pathways of a wilted, frozen garden, praying they might lose the wolves there.

Bare, rigid hedges lined the nearest pathway that Tilly led them down. Penelope did her best to keep up with the nimble fox, but she was already worn from her ordeal in the maze, and she could hear the scrabble of the wolves' claws against the paving stones as they closed in. She risked a glance back; one wolf was directly behind, while the other sought to head them off to the right.

With a frustrated growl, Tilly took a sharp turn onto a curving path that, she hoped, would help them lose their pursuers.

But the wolves never missed a step and Penelope was left with the uncomfortable feeling that their pursuers were herding them. The feeling only hardened into belief when they reached an enclosed grotto that offered no escape. Penelope and Tilly whirled round to face the wolves, nearly stumbling into a shallow pool as they did.

But their growls had ceased; indeed, their whole demeanor had utterly changed. Neither creature made a move to attack but walked forward slowly, cautiously. Tilly's fur remained bristled in anticipation nonetheless, but Penelope no longer believed there was cause for such wariness.

Hesitantly, the wolf nearest Penelope came closer, gauging her reaction with each careful step. Penelope stayed perfectly still, not wanting to alarm him.

With a few more steps, the wolf collapsed at her feet. Each ragged breath caused a crack to emerge in his stone frame, and Penelope knelt down, placing a tentative hand on the wolf's side. His companion came to lie down next to him, whining as he did so and offering Penelope another pleading look. Both creatures looked near to exhaustion as they lay panting, empty of what little fight had driven them to chase Penelope and Tilly to the pool.

"Don't fall for it, lass."

Penelope gave Tilly a reproving look. "If they meant to harm us, they would have done so by now." She looked down at both wolves once more. "They're tired, Tilly. We have to help them."

She glanced around the grotto, wondering what on earth you offered to refresh creatures made of stone. Briefly, Penelope lost her balance and stumbled a few steps into the pool.

"Water!"

Tilly cocked her head at the sudden exclamation.

"They need a drink," Penelope said as she cupped her hands into the cold water and quickly offered it to the wolf who had first collapsed at her feet. The creature raised his head just enough to lap up the water before the effort proved too much, and his stone muzzle returned to the ground.

Penelope repeated the gesture with the second wolf and waited. What she expected to happen, Penelope Grace did not know, but she anticipated something good nonetheless.

Hope like that does not disappoint.

The stone of the wolves' bodies began to crumble, proving to have only imprisoned the flesh and blood beneath. With every bit of unforgiving rock that was reduced to dust, the wolves' breathing grew fuller and deeper, their burden lighter, until both creatures were utterly free of it, just as they were created to be.

The transformation was a wondrous thing to witness, and Penelope Grace smiled in appreciation as the wolves playfully circled one another, barking in delight at their newfound freedom.

Tilly, however, let out a warning bark. The wolves stopped their prancing, but only for a moment.

With a mischievous snap at Tilly's tail, one of them said, "Don't you think our freedom is cause to celebrate, fox?"

"I've known ye since ye were a wee cub, Baren. Ye best show me some respect." Tilly pawed at the snow indignantly. "Fox, indeed!"

Baren fell silent, doing a terrible job of masking his amusement. For a moment, even in this dark place, Penelope Grace had to resist the urge to laugh.

True to form, though, Tilly's bristling tone only lasted a moment, and she soon looked at the wolves with a warmer gaze. "Aye, but it's good to see ye both again."

Before anything more could be said, the clouds above them began to darken, and a deep rumble shook the snowy ground. The smile faded from Penelope's face as she wondered if it were merely the weather or a sign that Denagon knew of their arrival and his recent loss of two slaves. Though she fervently wished it to be the former, Penelope knew better.

It was Tilly who broke the suddenly strained silence. "We need to move. The longer we stay here, the less chance we have of leavin'."

She received no argument, but as Baren and Penelope moved to follow Tilly, the second wolf, Loren, hung back with a low whine.

Baren turned. "Loren?"

"What about our pack, Baren? They've thought us dead all this time, and they don't know what Denagon can do." Loren turned an intelligent eye on Tilly. "You wouldn't be here unless you had a hope of defeating him, so war must be looming."

"Aye."

"Baren, shouldn't we warn them?"

Baren was silent for a moment. When next he spoke, he looked to Tilly. "Will you be all right without our aid?"

The fox raised a brow. "Have ye forgotten my name?"

Baren's bright blue eyes lit up once more with a smile. "Battle-mighty."

"Yer brother's right. Warn yer people, and we'll be seein' ye again soon."

Loren let out a parting bark before running for the gates, but Baren turned to Penelope first, nudging his muzzle beneath her hand. "Thank you. Your kindness softened what nothing else could," he said and was gone.

She felt suddenly lonely once they'd gone, though she agreed that their pack must be warned. Yet, just as a sliver of fear began to dampen her inner flame, a fresh breeze blew gently against her back before flowing through the garden.

Penelope Grace closed her eyes, and listened to the ice crackling on the branches in the winter garden. She looked up at Svarthol's imposing obsidian walls and was not afraid. Just as the ice only encased the trees for a time, allowing them to grow all the fuller come spring, the darkness that bound Leitad was only a passing thing.

You see, reader, this is what you must remember about darkness: however overpowering and victorious it may seem, darkness only ever shows off the Light's glory and brilliance.

The interior of Svarthol was deathly still and oppressively dark. Penelope and Tilly wandered its winding corridors with trepidation; Penelope found herself holding her breath as they came to each corner, fully expecting Denagon's creatures or Denagon himself to be waiting for them.

Their presence in Svarthol was no secret, after all. Penelope Grace knew that the maze and the now-free wolves were of Denagon's design, meant to deter and frighten her at the least or kill her at the worst.

She shuddered at the thought. Never would Penelope have believed that anyone, let alone a mysterious power from another world, would be anticipating how they might kill her. It simply wasn't something that happened to sixteen-year-old young women who live on quiet, snowy streets in England.

Yet, here she was, and there was no denying that Denagon would rejoice in killing her.

She would not make it easy for him.

They came to a large hall with tall glass doors on the left that opened up on the gardens. Penelope ran her fingers across the dusty cloth of a long dining table, covered in long-forgotten place settings that dully reflected what light entered through the windows.

On the opposite wall hung an ornate silver mirror; it was horribly tarnished – faded like everything else – but Penelope paused, all the same, to take in the room. For all the dust and neglect, she could still imagine this space in all its warm splendor, before the darkness laid claim to it.

A sharp whine from Tilly brought her back to the present moment, and Penelope glanced sharply at the fox, worried what the noise might attract.

Tilly's attention, however, was fixed on an old grandfather clock at the far end of the room. It stood next to a rather plain entryway, and on the top rested a large clockwork owl. The clock began to mark the hour. With each chime, an echo seemed to sound through the whole of Svarthol. The owl's burnished wings slowly outstretched with every turn of the gear, and as if in answer to the clock's announcement, complete darkness began to fall.

Penelope shuddered, but she could not look away from the unadorned entryway next to the clock. Something troubled her about it. Darkness was, indeed, falling, but the darkness gathering beyond the door was unnatural, too deep to be attributed to the setting of the sun.

She whispered Tilly's name, but the fox persisted in staring fixedly at the clock, and Penelope could not pull her attention away.

But they needed to leave, of that Penelope was sure. Something was not right, and they could not stand idle in the room, waiting for whatever fresh terror Denagon was preparing for them.

Scuffing her knee against the faded carpet in her rush, Penelope Grace knelt in front of Tilly, forcing the fox to look her in the eye. "Tilly, what is it? We need to leave. Now!"

The fox's eyes cleared, but when she spoke, she still seemed to be elsewhere. "Bartholomew," Tilly whispered, looking back to the owl, whom Penelope now understood was much more than a creature of cogs and gears. Tilly continued. "He saved me in the first battle. I thought he died. Now, I know he's alive, but seein' him enslaved in this way," she finished, her voice bitter and broken, "it's no comfort."

Heedless of the vanishing time, Penelope wrapped her arms around the fox and held her close. Pulling away, she held Tilly's gaze with all the fierce belief she could muster. "He will not be that way for long. He will know freedom before we take a step beyond Svarthol's gates."

"Aye, that he will," Tilly answered, her voice low, but less despairing than before.

"Now, I've had enough of his games," Penelope said, fire in her voice. "We need to find Denagon. You know this place. Where might he be waiting?"

"There are countless places to hide here." The fox paused, thinking. "Maybe the tower? He would've seen us leave the forest from there."

"Which way to the tower?"

Tilly glanced at the far doorway, the darkness ink-black, as if it was seeping into the room. "Through there."

Penelope's mouth set in a resigned line. "I ought to have known you'd say that."

But there was nothing for it, and so through the darkness, they went.

He had intended to toy with the wretch as she wound her way through his fortress, tease her into believing, just for a moment, that she might actually reach him and succeed. He had been enjoying every moment of his manipulation so far.

But just as the girl and the fox were passing into the darkness waiting beyond the doorway, a thought came to Denagon, a delicious possibility, and he knew he was right.

The girl sought to restore light; instead, she would be its undoing.

Penelope and Tilly passed beneath the door frame, and instantly, the passageway felt colder. This was a far cry from the high-ceilinged hallways they first passed through, even with all their winding turns.

This place was all cobbled stone and shadows, and Penelope kept losing her footing as she glanced behind, for she could not shake the feeling that they were being followed. They had not gone far, and already, she could barely make out the entranceway, as if the shadows were closing in behind them, shutting the way out.

Penelope thought she heard a whisper, almost like a sigh, pass by her, but when she whirled around, there was nothing to be seen. A few seconds later, Tilly stopped abruptly in the middle of the passageway.

"Did you see something?" Penelope whispered.

The fox pricked up her ears, listening, and did not answer at first. Then, "This doesn't feel right. We need to turn back."

"But Tilly, Denagon –."

"Don't argue! This is too easy. Now, follow me."

Disgruntled though she was, Penelope trusted Tilly's instincts, and so, back down the corridor they went. As they returned, the shadows seemed to lift away like cobwebs suddenly removed after long years of being forgotten. But the pit in Penelope's stomach only grew. Still, she did not argue with Tilly again, and the doorway soon came into sight.

They were passing beneath it when a familiar figure blocked their way. Penelope stopped dead in her tracks. It was like being back in the forest, frozen, unable to escape from its flat, dead eyes.

The wisp-thin robe, tattered as ever, seemed to float about the sickly frame as the figure reached for Penelope. Only this time, she was given a moment of clarity. Penelope Grace remembered what it had cost her friends to save her in the forest, and before Tilly could put herself at risk, Penelope grabbed the fox in her arms and bolted back down the passage.

The figure shrieked in rage, and Tilly wrestled against Penelope's grip, but she refused to let go. Not once did she look back. A rush of bitterly cold wind blew against her back, and Penelope knew the creature followed them, but there was a staircase coming up to their left, and if they could just make it, perhaps they could escape.

A few more feet and she was climbing the stairs two at a time. Breathless as she was, Penelope Grace pushed herself on until they came to the staircase's end and the tower room. Tilly wriggled out of her grasp at last just before Penelope slammed the door shut behind them.

She was greeted by bristling fur and bared teeth from Tilly. "Fool of a girl!"

"You might thank me," she retorted, instantly defensive.

"Thank ye? We've nowhere to run because of yer rashness!"

"We escaped because of me!"

Tilly growled in vicious aggravation. "Don't ye find it the least bit odd that we weren't kept from comin' in, but from leavin'? Or that all it took was a wee bit of a run down the hallway to escape one of the most powerful creatures Denagon has in his keepin'?"

"We were led here, girl. And now we're trapped."

Penelope Grace was stunned and humiliated. What a fool she had been. But there was no opportunity for her to stammer out an apology. Her attention was pulled away by the faintest of smoke pouring in beneath the doorway.

It circled the room, growing denser by the moment, and Tilly let out a warning growl as she watched it encircle them.

After a moment, the smoke around the perimeter of the circular room began to work its way closer to the pair, freezing the stone it left in its wake. The ice started to crawl up the walls, and Penelope knew with unflinching certainty who was coming for them.

The shadow gathered in the center of the room, deepening and rising, until Denagon stood before Penelope Grace, pleased beyond imagining by how easy she had been to manipulate.

She could only stare, horrified by the very same thought, and unable to comprehend how she was meant to defeat Denagon, now that he stood before her.

"You are a long way from home, little girl," Denagon said quietly, and she flinched at the way his voice slithered into her thoughts.

"You hurt my family." She meant to sound fierce and indignant, but her words spilled out, barely above a whisper.

The shadows deepened around Denagon as he drew closer. "I would have done much more than that," he said. Slowly, he reached out a pale hand as if to stroke the side of Penelope's face, but he stopped just shy of touching her, and anger filled his eyes.

Turning away in frustration, he stalked around the room, never taking his eyes off of her.

Penelope, tired of his games, gathered up some courage and spoke. "What purpose do you think it will serve to lock me away in here? Even if you kill me, do you think that can stop the Light?"

Denagon hissed in answer as if struck, but the next second, a sly look crept into his eyes. "You speak brazenly for one who knows so little. Had I known my enemy sent me such a worthy adversary, I would have greeted you with more respect." With that, he took a mocking bow.

Penelope Grace burned with anger, but helplessness raged right beside it. She had Denagon right in front of her. Now, how was she meant to stop him?

He read the question in her eyes with delight and pounced.

"You seem unsure of yourself. I can hardly blame you. It's unthinkable that He would send someone so young to even contain the darkness, let alone destroy it."

Penelope Grace took a steadying breath. She knew he was trying to undermine her; still, every doubt he voiced, she had wondered.

Tilly had been observing from the moment Denagon appeared, hoping he would forget her in his fixation on Penelope.

Her patience was soon rewarded.

There was more to this than they understood, she knew. But she did not understand what. She needed to listen and wait, so she stayed quiet even when Penelope made a poor attempt at bravado. She knew that Denagon was baiting Penelope, but Tilly also knew that she needed him to if she hoped to catch him in a mistake.

Keep him talking long enough, and he was bound to make one.

It came sooner than Tilly expected, but she caught it instantly.

She barked out a warning, hoping against hope that Penelope might realize Denagon's plan, but he anticipated her, and Tilly's vision went dark.

"Tilly!" Penelope shouted as the fox went limp against the wall.

Denagon spared no more than a glance at the intuitive, now useless, little fox.

He had her now, with no friends left to help her see clearly.

"Tell me, girl, were you really meant to come here? After all, what hope do you now have left? You are friendless now, and your family is dead."

"They are *not* dead," Penelope Grace shouted, unable to keep quiet any longer.

But Denagon was untroubled, his response needling. "How do you know?" he asked, circling her once again. "Frozen beneath the ice, how long could they last?"

She closed her eyes tightly and clenched her fists, trying to shut him out.

She failed.

Denagon stopped just behind her. "Tell me, even if He brought you here, what has He really done for you since all this began?"

Though Penelope could not see it, Denagon's smile was wicked. For every seed of doubt he planted, her determination grew, and she would fight back just as he anticipated.

Her eyes were still shut, but a fire of brightest flame was growing within Penelope Grace. No matter how persuasive his words, he was a liar and nothing more. She would not allow him to frighten her into turning back now. There was too much at stake for her own world, as well as for Ellura and its people.

Penelope Grace opened her eyes wide to what is true.

"He stopped you from claiming me."

Denagon flinched but did not back down. "Speak up, girl," he taunted.

Penelope turned to face him, head held high, and gaze steady. "He stopped you from claiming me," she repeated, then went on, for she realized that for every attack she had suffered, an unlikely, impossibly real rescue had taken place.

"He ensured that an empty locket came into my care. And when I was without hope, He brought a wolf to lead me to another world."

A splinter of light broke through the shadows at Denagon's side, and he hunched over, staggering away from her. Penelope advanced, made bold by his weakening. "When your creatures came against my friends and me on our journey, He caused each one to fail."

The cracks in the darkness grew, illuminating the room. The ice covering the tower walls began to drip. Outside, the sound of running water came to Penelope's ears, soft now, but growing triumphantly louder.

"Before I ever asked for a way out, He showed me the way through a maze."

Denagon gave a pained cry and fell to his hands and knees. The light continued to grow in intensity, and he was clearly weakening, yet he seemed to take the wounds with a strange relish. Penelope Grace hesitated for the briefest moment, and when she did, Denagon met her eyes.

At first, his gaze seemed defiant, but as the light became more brilliant, and the sound of running water grew louder, Penelope Grace felt something expectant in the way he looked at her. Was all this a trick, she briefly allowed herself to wonder, but she quickly pushed the thought away, allowing it no traction.

She would not let his creeping doubt undermine her purpose now. Not when she was so close to defeating him.

Penelope Grace knelt down next to him, untroubled by the Light's brilliance. "He freed your slaves and revealed them to be friends. And against all the odds, I have the strength to defeat you."

A great rumble shook the earth at her words, and to her horror, Denagon began to laugh, even as the Light eradicated the shadows around him. Though each word was an effort, he managed to spit out a triumphant, "You foolish wretch," before the Light seemed to banish him utterly.

Briefly, Penelope shielded her eyes from the brilliance, but the light soon returned to normal, and when next she looked, sunlight was filtering into the tower. But she felt no sense of victory.

Something was wrong.

Penelope Grace rushed to the tower's window, letting out a despairing cry as she gripped the stone ledge to keep herself steady. Light had, indeed, been restored to Leitad, but beyond its gates, a sight greeted Penelope that she could not have anticipated.

Darkness was falling on Ellura, overshadowing and oppressing all things, like a devouring hell.

What had she done?

Denagon was exultant as he sped across the land in the company of shadows. His slaves surrounded him on all sides, setting forests ablaze and seeking out victims as the unnatural darkness fell around them.

Could it have been more glorious?

A perverse laugh escaped him as he watched the dominion he had long dreamed of fall on the land.

Long he had sought to claim Ellura for his own, and he had believed his victory secure once Leitad became his. But once he had driven the Light's followers out, he had found to his frustration that his encompassing darkness could not pass beyond its borders.

He had thought that killing the girl was the only way of remedying his captivity, only to find that she was the very key to his freedom.

He supposed that it wasn't really so surprising. Carriers of Apricity though they might be, humans never had liked surrender; they preferred to feel that true strength came from them, and it always proved their downfall.

"Tilly, wake up!" Penelope Grace pleaded, shaking the fox's shoulder.

Slowly, the fox began to stir, but she felt disoriented and ached all over from her impact with the stone wall. "What happened?" Tilly managed while trying to get her bearings.

She looked around, noticing the sudden airiness of the tower; instantly, she sprang to alertness. "Where is Denagon?"

Penelope Grace looked down, her hands shaking for fear of speaking the words, of owning her own failure. Tilly's harsh rebuke before her confrontation with Denagon was still painfully fresh, and she did not feel able to face another wave of disappointment from the fox, whom she had come to care so dearly for.

Still, the words must be said, no matter how ineloquent they might be. "Tilly, I failed. Whatever Apricity I might carry, it's not enough. I'm not enough." Penelope Grace paused before forcing herself to say the rest. "He's taking over Ellura, Tilly. Along with all his creatures."

Tilly blinked once, not seeming able to absorb the news. Penelope could not meet her eye. Then all of a sudden, the fox sprang up, racing to the windowsill, as if only now comprehending what Penelope's words truly meant.

With her paws on the ledge, Tilly looked out on the land below. Within Leitad's gates, all was crisp, yet golden. A pure snowfall blanketed the castle's grounds, and everything shimmered with newness. Winter foliage grew, fresh and vibrant, and the sun's rays set everything ablaze.

But beyond, all was darkness and disorder, stark and barren. Gloom and shadow had stripped winter of its often-overlooked life, and far in the distance, Tilly could see the dance of fire as the forest began to fall to its flames.

"We must help them," Tilly said, refusing to be daunted by Denagon's rampage.

"What is there to be done?" Penelope asked, her voice low and despondent.

With a snarl, Tilly snapped her jaws at the girl, sending Penelope jumping back, startled by the sudden show of anger. "Ye can stop feelin' sorry for yerself to start!" the fox barked. "Ye'll help no one that way."

Penelope Grace stared at Tilly with wide eyes, knowing she was right, but so terrified by the repercussions of her failure that she could find no words to say.

Seeing her fear, Tilly's bristled fur softened. "I'm sorry, Penelope. But I've got no time to comfort ye. We must run and run hard. Are ye still willin'?" she asked, a familiar gleam in her eyes.

The faintest shadow of a smile broke through Penelope's gloom. She whispered, "Yes."

And they ran.

Shall we follow them?

They crouched behind Leitad's gates, uncertain of what waited immediately beyond their protection. Beyond the borders of the reclaimed fortress, darkness reigned, and while neither Tilly nor Penelope Grace could see any of Denagon's slaves, that did not mean they were not waiting out of sight.

Through the gloom of the land facing them, Penelope could barely make out the entrance to the maze, and she could not pretend to relish the thought of walking its paths again. "Is there no other way, Tilly?"

"I'm afraid not. I dare not risk goin' round. We've no way of knowin' how far it stretches, and we cannot afford to lose the time."

Penelope nodded, resigning herself to the idea. She was just about to leave their hiding place when looking ahead, she saw the light reflect off a pair of eyes watching them from the maze.

"Tilly," Penelope breathed with a nod to the maze. It was too late to pretend that she hadn't noticed the watcher; they had locked eyes, and Penelope Grace imagined that, whatever manner of beast it might be, such simple tricks would not work on it.

"Aye, I see it," the fox responded, her muscles bunching beneath her fur. "Stay here, girl."

This time, Penelope did not argue. They were blessed to have seen their enemy before abandoning their shelter, but they could not see what they faced clearly through the fog, and she knew Tilly was their best chance of escaping.

The fox crept forward, a low growl of challenge sounding from the back of her throat.

An answering growl came, much lower than Tilly's, and Penelope readied herself to help Tilly if needed. But the fox seemed unconcerned. Steadily, she continued forward, her focus never wavering from the watcher in the mist.

Then suddenly, a new attacker, hidden by the fog until now, lunged at Tilly from outside of the maze. Tilly was ready, though, as if she had known all along that this second creature was the real danger. The fox darted to the right, then back beneath her opponent's legs, snapping at its heels.

The creature stumbled, and before Penelope could blink, Tilly had her teeth bared threateningly at its throat.

But nothing happened.

And then a familiar, low laugh sounded from across the way.

Penelope Grace's heart nearly stopped beating from relief when Elafry emerged from the maze, and she ran to meet her friends.

Tilly stepped back from the rising form beneath her, clearly pleased with herself. "Ye always did underestimate me, wolf."

"I didn't notice you managing to wound me," Aira retorted as she regained her feet.

"No, ye're right about that," Tilly remarked with a laugh. "Ye only tripped."

Aira let out a disgruntled growl in answer, though Penelope knew she wasn't genuinely agitated. But Tilly was not done gloating.

"Oh, come now, Aira, we both know that if I'd thought ye were one of Denagon's creatures, ye'd not be walkin'."

"How could you see me through the mist?"

"I didn't. But I'd recognize Elafry's blue eyes anywhere. And besides," the fox continued with a sly grin, "I taught ye that trick."

Aira snorted. "You taught me no such thing," she insisted. Then, deciding the conversation was over, the wolf turned to Penelope. Her voice was warm when she spoke. "Penelope Grace, it is good to see you again."

Penelope knelt, putting her arms around the wolf, before shifting back to look at her. "Oh, Aira. Nothing's gone as we planned."

Aira gave her a comforting nudge with her muzzle. "Nothing ever does. But we don't give up because of it."

A shriek sounded above them, and they looked up to find several of Denagon's winged servants circling in the sky nearby.

"Into the maze, now," Aira said, and Penelope Grace, along with her companions, returned to its twisting paths once more.

"Aira," Penelope Grace asked, "what has happened since we were separated?"

The small company had been making their way through the maze for some time now. Though the vines had ceased writhing and nothing troubled them, the maze was still vast. All the same, Penelope marveled at how much more quickly she might have passed through it had she followed the illuminated lanterns.

In answer, Aira replied, "Much. After we were separated, some of the beasts pursued you; we trusted Tilly to keep you safe. Elafry and I were able to fend off or evade the others, and once dawn approached, the most relentless of them, at last, gave up the chase.

"We both knew that Denagon's forces would not be massing so far from Svarthol unless he was planning an attack on our peoples. We went in search of Elafry's people, hoping to give them a warning that they might pass on to Arabella before time ran out; we found Copernicus instead."

"Is he all right?" Penelope interrupted eagerly. "What of Wynnfelde? Did you find Eloise and Frederick, as well?"

Aira chuckled. "Yes, we found them all, though not so quickly as all that. Some distance downriver, the beast that attacked Eloise dragged her from the river, but that proved a mistake. Copernicus told us later that he outpaced Wynnfelde and, reaching the creature first, made swift work of killing it.

"Frederick was still captive to the river, but Wynnfelde succeeded, with great effort, in keeping him safe. All the same, she and Copernicus knew they were all much too weak to regain us. Copernicus, as it happens, had the same thought we did; Elafry's people live throughout the forest, and they would provide shelter.

"He continued on to find help and found Elafry and I. Once we were certain that Arabella and all those in the stronghold would be warned, we turned back once more to find you. Copernicus and Wynnfelde wait in the forest for us. Frederick and Eloise remained behind. Since that time, I do not know what has happened or if our warning did, indeed, reach Arabella swiftly enough."

Her tale ended, Aira fell silent. Penelope Grace did not give any answer at first. She kept thinking of the many sacrifices everyone was making, all because of the belief that she would be able to defeat Denagon and free Ellura from his snare. So many were putting themselves in harm's way, and so far, she had done nothing to warrant such trust.

Penelope slowed her steps, letting Tilly and Elafry move ahead of them. Though still hesitant, she said softly, "Aira, everyone believes that I can save them. But what if I can't? I fought Denagon, though not physically. I spoke of all the ways that He's been faithful to me since this began, and it seemed to work, but at the last..." Her voice died to a whisper. "Aira, I failed. Denagon was driven out of Leitad, but unleashed on the rest of Ellura."

Aira looked thoughtfully at Penelope before speaking. "May I ask what was said when you confronted Denagon?"

"I spoke of how He led me here, how He brought me through the maze... I told him that I had the strength to defeat him."

Aira was quiet for what seemed an unbearably long time to Penelope. "Aira?" she at last prompted.

The wolf stopped in the middle of the path, meeting the girl's pleading eyes. "Think on it, Penelope Grace. It will mean more if you come to understand it for yourself."

With that, Aira moved ahead, leaving Penelope to contemplate her words while she rejoined the others. Penelope continued on but at a slower pace. What could she have done differently in the face of such an enemy, she wondered, but there was no time left to dwell on the question. Around the next turn was the way out, and Tilly called for her to catch up.

Only a short distance from where they stood, the forest waited. There was no movement nearby, but Penelope Grace could hear the calls and cries of their enemies far off, wreaking untold havoc as they swarmed over Ellura.

Penelope crouched down next to Aira, quietly as she could. In a barely audible whisper, Aira said, "Wynnfelde and Copernicus are waiting for us in the forest."

Still, the wolf made no move to leave the cover of the maze as Penelope asked, "Do you think that something else waits for us?"

"Yes. Copernicus was meant to keep watch and signal to me. If he's made no sign, it means there's trouble."

"What do we do?"

Aira glanced over at Penelope with a mischievous look. "We go and make some of our own."

For all the tension of the moment, Penelope Grace could not help but grin at Aira's pluck. "Are we all ready?" she asked, looking back at Tilly and Elafry.

Both fox and lion nodded, and together, they ran.

The second they left the shelter of the maze, attackers burst from the trees, surging towards them, and all was chaos and confusion. Penelope Grace rushed ahead, her feet seeming to fly across cold earth as she followed Tilly into the forest.

Though slowed by their enemies, this time, Aira and Elafry were able to overcome them, and there was no separation of their company.

The barren trees flashed by. Aira led the way, heading for some unknown place, but she stopped abruptly in a small clearing where Penelope guessed they had left Copernicus and Wynnfelde.

But neither of their friends were there, and they could not afford to linger. Already their enemies were in pursuit.

Penelope Grace looked up and saw winged creatures swooping down from above the trees. They dashed away, continuing their mad race. Determinedly, Penelope kept pace with them, but after everything she had endured, she feared how long she could last. Her body desperately needed rest.

But the cries of their enemies were close behind. A prayer was offered up, exhaustion temporarily kept at bay, and the small company continued to flee through the gloom.

They collapsed in the early morning of the third day, hoping that the light, dim though it was, would deter their pursuers. Penelope's breath came in quick gasps, and a sharp pain in her side caused her to wince every time she breathed in.

Both the wolf and the fox watched her closely, but it was Aira who spoke. "You can't continue like this, Penelope Grace. None of us can," Aira concluded, glancing at Tilly and Elafry. "We need to find Copernicus and Wynnfelde."

"And how d'ye reckon we'll do that, Aira?" Tilly asked. "They could be anywhere, and we canna afford to turn back now. We need to find our camp."

"Which is equally impossible, Tilly," Aira snapped. "Would you happen to know where to start looking?" The fox was silent. "I thought not."

"Stop it, both of you," Penelope interjected. "You're both right. We cannot leave our friends behind, but we must find Ellura's fighting force. All of us need rest, and then, Aira, you should try to track Copernicus and Wynnfelde while we continue our search for the camp."

At this, Aira pressed her forehead against Penelope's. "I will not leave you again, Penelope Grace."

"Nor should you," Elafry said. "The idea of separating does not sit well with me, no matter how noble our reasons. We must remain together and trust that Wynnfelde and Copernicus will be reunited with us at the right time."

The lion's words hung in the silence, wise and final. With only a few more words exchanged, they were all agreed and lay down to rest in shifts.

Several hours passed before it was Penelope's turn to keep watch. It would not be long before the day passed into evening. Exhausted still, she leaned back against a nearby tree to watch and to wait.

She expected no trouble. Denagon's creatures were the least active during the daylight hours, shadowy and gloomy though they were, and it was their one opportunity to rest. Still, she remained watchful for the first two hours.

But the time passed slowly, and for all her efforts, Penelope's eyes began to close.

Seconds later, a soft blue light flashed between two trees some distance in front of her, and Penelope jerked awake. She watched, staying perfectly still, until she saw it again, closer this time.

Frowning, Penelope observed the light for a few more moments, making sure that the fast-approaching dusk was not playing tricks on her. Then she whispered, "Aira," and the wolf was at her side in a moment.

"Look," Penelope continued quietly. "Is that what I think it is?"

"A snow sprite," Aira confirmed, the relief in her eyes evident. "Wait here with the others."

Slowly, the wolf padded her way through the crisp snow. Penelope watched, desperately hoping that the sprite had been sent by one of their friends or, at least, had some news of them. Aira spoke with the sprite for what seemed an age to Penelope and then returned alone.

They woke Tilly and Elafry before Aira would share what she had learned. "The snow sprite, Aralie, is not alone," she said. "Several of them wait further on. She will lead us to them, but we must hurry. Arabella and the others abandoned the stronghold so that Ellura's forces would not be divided. There is a camp not far from here, but Aralie says that Denagon's army is working to encircle it. We have little time left to reach it."

"Then let us run," Tilly said decidedly and bolted in the direction of the waiting sprite.

Elafry followed her, and Penelope moved to do the same, but Aira stepped in front of her, blocking her path. "You must answer me honestly, Penelope Grace. Can you run this final stretch?"

"Yes," Penelope replied, and no hesitation lingered in her answer.

With a nod, Aira ran, and Penelope followed.

The companions were just reaching the rise of a crisp snowbank when the other snow sprites appeared, speaking so quickly in their small voices that Penelope Grace failed to catch the words. But Aralie understood their warning, and she turned to the others. "Denagon's creatures are ahead, moving to cut us off. They must have spotted us from above. We must change course. Follow me!"

She darted to the right, and they rushed to keep pace with her as she flew ahead. Penelope could hardly breathe for the biting wind and her own exhaustion. Her legs felt weak beneath her, but she pushed on, knowing that if she could reach the camp, she could rest. But the thought of rest only made her feel more sluggish, and she stumbled despite her best efforts.

Immediately, Aira was there, speaking encouraging words and helping her to stand once more. "Think of Georgie, Penelope Grace. Think of your family, and run with me."

With a ragged breath, she nodded, praying that the camp was not far and that her feet would carry her the distance. She barely made it several paces before a cry sounded from above, alerting them all to the presence of Denagon's winged slaves.

Penelope risked a glance up just as the creature swooped down towards her. Though she dodged in time, its jagged claws snagged on the hood of her cloak, and she lost her balance in the deepening snow.

Scrambling to her feet as the creature screamed in frustration, Penelope whirled around to face the next attack just as the snow sprites shot past her. Penelope Grace's eyes widened as she watched their remarkable work, unaware until now what the sprites were capable of.

Before her, a wall of thick, swirling snow appeared, blinding the enemies pursuing from behind and affording Penelope and her companions safe passage, if only for a short time.

Aralie came to hover before Penelope's eyes. "Hurry now! The camp is not far from here, but the further away we fly, the more fragile the wall will become."

With that, they were off. Penelope could see Elafry and the others racing ahead of her through the trees. They ran a great distance, yet Penelope still saw no sign of the camp. The trees nearby looked hazy, and it was not long before she could hardly make them out at all. In fact, the whole forest about her was fading from sight, hidden by a blanketing of white.

Nevertheless, she could clearly see the faint blue light of the snow sprites flying just ahead, which proved enough. Moments later, the snow sprites halted, and the others along with them. Penelope Grace could see nothing but white in front of them, and for a moment, she could not comprehend what she was looking at.

Understanding came in a flash. Though the snow was spinning so quickly that it seemed to be at a standstill, moving it was, in an impossibly high wall in front of them. It was similar to the wall of snow that the sprites had conjured to throw off their pursuers, but what rose before them seemed altogether impenetrable in comparison.

Briefly, Penelope caught sight of flickering blue light through the swirling snow. "What is this, Aralie?" she asked.

The snow sprite flew so near to Penelope that she could feel the breeze created by her beating wings. "This is our camp, Penelope, hidden by snow. No slave of the enemy can pass through this wall. You and your friends may pass through without fear."

Tilly trotted through with no hesitation, her courage undaunted by the impressive sight. Penelope, however, remained still. Noticing her hesitation, Aralie said, "The snow will not harm you. It only prevents our enemies from entering." And with that, the snow sprite flitted through the snow, as if to prove the truthfulness of her words.

Taking a deep breath, Penelope Grace passed through the snow. For a minute, the world was purest white, and then she stepped through into a sprawling camp that must have stretched two miles at least.

Everyone from the stronghold was here, and more. Fires were blazing at regular intervals, and the smell of warm food soon reached her. Penelope Grace nearly collapsed with relief. The war against Denagon was far from over, but for the moment, she was surrounded by friends and roaring fires, and she was safe.

The morning dawned, seeming brighter to Penelope Grace than it had in many days. She woke to the bustle of movement and found that Ellura's people were busily fortifying the borders of the camp within the wall of snow.

She rose with a deep stretch, relishing the unfamiliar experience of waking rested and went in search of Arabella and her friends. The Ismey turned out to be the easiest to find. She stood at the north end of the camp, discussing defenses with a small group of people. Penelope was momentarily startled by the sight of fellow humans. She had not come across any others like herself since arriving here, and though their presence wasn't unwelcome, it was surprising after so many days spent in the company of countless other beings.

She remained somewhat distant from the group, not wanting to intrude on the conversation. After a few moments, Arabella noticed her waiting and brought the conversation to a close. One of the men talking with her, an older gentleman, perhaps in his early seventies, turned around to walk beside Arabella. When he looked up at Penelope Grace, however, the man froze where he stood, letting out a sharp exhale as he did so.

She was caught by his gaze, his eyes a clear, startling blue, so full of sadness and something else that she couldn't quite explain. Neither of them said a word, and neither of them moved. For a long moment, they stayed just like this, until Arabella broke in, saying, "Fahren, please guide the others while they work. We have little time left."

He jumped at her voice, then responded in a deep, kindly voice, "Of course, Arabella. I'll be on the south end if you have need of me."

He cast one final look at Penelope Grace and was gone, walking with steady determination as if he had to force himself to move forward and not take one last glance at the girl.

Immediately, Penelope turned to the Ismey, a question ready on her lips, but Arabella held up a hand to stop her, though her voice was kind. "I know what you will ask, Penelope Grace, but it is not yet time for that story. I have something I want to give you. Follow me."

Penelope did not argue; though the unanswered question burned within her, what could she say? The time for the battle against Denagon was nearly upon them, and Arabella was right. That alone must be their focus now.

The Ismey led her to one of many tents, no different from any of the others. Inside was only a modest pile of blankets and a large leather bag.

From this, Arabella retrieved a long dagger in a beautiful pearlescent sheath.

"I should have given this to you from the start. Foolishly, I thought the protection of your companions would be enough to keep you safe. For that error, you have my apology, Penelope Grace."

Carefully, she passed the blade to the uncertain young woman, who had only ever dreamed of swordplay. As Penelope took the dagger in hand, Arabella continued, "Your grandmother once carried this blade. It will not serve you against Denagon himself, but against his creatures, it will afford you at least some protection."

Penelope stared at the blade for several seconds, wondering what its history might be and brimming with thankfulness to have at least this small part of her grandmother with her. She looked back up at Arabella. "Thank you."

A small smile graced the Ice Maiden's features. "You are most welcome." Her smile faltered. "We have no time to teach you how to wield this weapon. Time is slipping from us."

Penelope frowned. "What is our plan? How are we to fight off Denagon's forces?"

A brief pause, then, "The snow sprites will lower the wall in two days."

"Two days?" Penelope nearly shouted, incredulous. "How could we possibly be prepared in so little time?"

Arabella's answer was both patient and kind. "It is no longer a matter of preparedness, Penelope. All the might Denagon can muster is encircling our camp, cutting us off from any further aid. While they cannot pass through the snow sprite's wall, neither can we eternally remain here. Better if we decide the time of our battle."

Penelope Grace stood silent, wrestling with the wisdom of Arabella's words and her own fear of facing Denagon once more. Finally, "And he will join his army soon?"

"He is already here."

Penelope looked up sharply, and this time, the Ice Maiden had no reassurance to give. "I can feel the darkness that he brings encircling us. Apart from Leitad, this camp is the last point of light in all of Ellura."

She could not speak, so shaken was she by the pervasiveness of the darkness and by how quickly it had overtaken this land. Thinking of it, Penelope could not keep herself from wondering if things would have gone differently had she never set foot in Svarthol.

Sensing, at least in part, Penelope's turmoil, Arabella reached out a comforting hand. "Find your friends, Penelope. Let them encourage and cheer you. I know the weight of this is immense, but I also know there is hope still."

She only managed a brief nod in answer before exiting the tent and wandering aimlessly through the camp.

The next two days passed by in a haze of preparation for others and confusion for Penelope Grace. Please do not misunderstand me, reader; Penelope helped where she could, refusing to sit idle because of her fear of the coming confrontation, but fear it she did.

All others in the camp seemed so assured to her eyes, so confident that they would meet their foes head-on, no matter the cost to themselves. And Penelope fully intended to join them in their efforts.

She thought not at all of turning back, only of failing.

As the hours passed, she became more and more convinced of her own inability to face Denagon and emerge victoriously. She was too weak, too inexperienced, too young. How could they ask this of her and expect any other outcome but defeat?

Denagon's power was too immense in comparison to her little strength, and whatever Apricity she carried, Penelope dared not believe that it was enough.

Even as she served alongside others, her thoughts swirled around this doubtful center, and her fear grew, and her faith dwindled.

Aira noticed the change in her but chose to wait still, knowing that it was something Penelope would have to understand in her own time. Tilly, likewise, noticed the girl's darkening mood and decided that enough was enough.

She plopped down next to Penelope Grace on the darkening evening of the second day and looked her squarely in the face. "Don't ye think it's high time to stop feelin' sorry for yerself?"

Penelope flinched at the reminder of the fox's harsh words in the tower room of Svarthol and had no answer for the bold fox.

Tilly pressed on, undeterred. "Well? What's troublin' ye so?"

She stared at Tilly for a moment more before the words flooded out, her words only whispered. "You said it yourself, Tilly. *Fool of a girl.* And you were right. It was foolish to barricade us in the tower, thinking we were safe, that I had somehow outsmarted him.

"It was foolish to believe that I could best him." She paused. "You should have seen it, Tilly, the way the darkness swept over the land."

For a moment, Penelope Grace stared into the fire before them, and Tilly waited, knowing they'd yet to reach the heart of the matter. "I was so relieved when we made it here, Tilly. But over the last two days, I find myself wondering. Our camp seems so large, and there are so many here who are willing to fight for Ellura. But having seen the darkness, having seen Denagon face-to-face, I can't help but wonder, is it enough? Am I?"

At this, Tilly's face took on a decidedly impatient look. "D'ye still not understand? This isna' about *ye*, girl."

Penelope looked over at her, startled and indignant. "I beg to differ. I was brought here because of my Apricity."

Tilly snorted. "Ye were brought here because of the Apricity ye were *given*." She fell silent briefly, thinking how best to explain; then, deciding, said, "Apricity isna' just light, Penelope Grace. It's a flame, placed within ye. Did ye think ye started that flame all on yer own? It didna' come from ye, child. It came from *Him*."

The fire crackled in the ensuing silence, but Tilly was not yet finished. "When the terrors of the night surround us, and all seems lost, it's Him who'll save us in the end. But what a wonder to be used by Him 'til He comes," she concluded, and her eyes were warm with the reflection of the firelight.

Having said her piece, Tilly rose and trotted off to another part of the camp. Penelope sat very still. Every despairing thought that had kept her company these past days had been unceremoniously illuminated by a bold young fox. Penelope Grace felt as though she had been standing in a horribly darkened room, only to shield her eyes from the sudden flooding in of light.

Morning dawned, and anticipation swelled within their camp. The snow sprites had reported the evening before that Denagon's creatures were steadily circling the camp, looking for a weakness and finding none. Little did their enemies expect that they did not intend to shield themselves much longer.

Not long after the camp rose, Aira found Penelope Grace buckling the belt for her dagger tightly around her waist. It took her a moment to notice the wolf standing nearby, but soon enough, Penelope looked up. They said nothing for a long moment, each gazing at the other.

Aira padded forward, nudging her head beneath Penelope's hand. "You will fight well, Penelope Grace."

A flash of nervousness passed across her face. "I have no idea how to wield a weapon, Aira, not really."

"Well, thank goodness it isn't that sword you will ultimately need."

Penelope smiled at Aira's riddles, struck suddenly by how fiercely she would miss the wolf and all her companions. Dangerous though Ellura was, a love for this place was planted in her; Penelope wondered how she would feel when the time came to leave behind a place that had captured a piece of her grandmother's heart and now, her own.

Aira, guessing her thoughts, said quietly, "We never know for certain, Penelope Grace, where we will be led or when, perhaps, we might be called to return to those places that have come to feel like home. We might see each other again."

"Oh, Aira," Penelope began, but no other words would have proved enough, and so, together in comfortable silence, the pair walked to join the others at the camp's borders.

All her companions stood nearby – Wynnfelde, with Eloise and Frederick not far behind, Copernicus and Elafry just behind herself and Aira, and Tilly at her right-hand side – and Penelope felt a good deal better with faithful friends standing beside her.

The fox looked up at her, a fierce, encouraging light in her eyes. "Stay close to me, child, as much as ye can." Tilly's gaze went to the wall as the snow sprites began to fly towards it. "And when the time comes to face yer foe, ye remember that ye're not as alone as that liar'd have ye believe."

With a nod and shaky breath, Penelope Grace looked forward and watched as the wall of snow began to fall.

Everything was chaos on the other side of the barricade, and Denagon reveled in it. Triumph was coming, at last, the time for darkness to reign, and all his creatures were mad with the anticipation of it.

He stood at the back of his army, content to let the dumb beasts go ahead of him, give their lives for darkness and shadow, while he chose the time to snatch the girl.

Denagon knew she waited on the other side, could feel the light within her burning far more intensely than he expected after her first defeat. Oh, how he hated the Light. With all the strength that was in him, he longed to smother it, feel it gutter out beneath his hands.

And this time, he would see it done.

Movement at the far end of the camp caught his attention, and Denagon's gaze snapped up.

It could not be.

But yes, he was sure. The wall was lowering, each infuriating snowflake falling to the earth like so much dust.

"Fools," he whispered, but a wicked gleam lit up his pale, flat eyes. "You glorious fools."

She stood frozen when the first bloodthirsty creature charged at her, but then Penelope Grace remembered. She remembered the way the ice had crept across Georgie's skin, stealing him — all her family — away from her, and she raised her grandmother's blade and ran forward with an emboldened cry.

The beast's face, all grey, cracking skin, leered down at her as their blades met. He bore down on her, impossibly strong, and Penelope knew she could not best him in strength. But perhaps…

Suddenly, she darted out of the way, while all the beast's power was brought to bear against thin air. He stumbled forwards, and Penelope slashed her dagger across the back of his legs to keep him from pursuing.

The roar of battle threatened to overwhelm her as she ran to meet Tilly, who faced the most enormous creature Penelope had yet seen, like a great ogre out of some legend. Together, they brought him down, while not far to their right, several snow sprites sent a blast of snow and ice to freeze an entire group of Denagon's slaves.

Penelope met the next three foes with great courage, all the while searching for Denagon in the madness. Some enemies she outwitted, while others she bested, much to her surprise. But still, they came, an endless stream of attackers, all devoted with incredible hatred to destroying Ellura and its peoples.

There seemed to be no end to Denagon's army. Though she would not turn back, with each raise of the blade, Penelope's arms grew heavier until they felt like a dead weight hanging from her exhausted frame.

A pained yelp sounded behind her, and Penelope whirled round to find Aira, some distance from her, pinned beneath the talons of a scaled beast, very much like a dragon, but with a twisted form that was terribly unlike the magnificent creatures of Penelope's dreams.

Penelope knelt in the snow, battling an impossible weariness, but still, she rose, determined to help her friend. She stumbled as she ran, but the distance was closing swiftly between herself and Aira, and if she could only reach her in time —

Stop.

The force of it shook Penelope Grace, and she so desperately wanted to disregard it, scoff at it as foolish, but she had heard His voice before and knew better now than to ignore it. And so, she stopped, not understanding, but nevertheless trusting that it was not, in fact, up to her to save her friend.

The next instant, a smaller, but no less fearsome, winged creature snatched Penelope Grace up by the shoulders, bearing her away from friend and foe alike.

She was dumped on the hard, frozen earth, and her body ached from the jarring impact. The dagger, she already knew, was lost to her, but Arabella had made it clear that the blade would not serve her against Denagon, and why else would she have been carried away from her friends?

With a groan, Penelope Grace rose to her feet, meeting his gaze as levelly as she could.

Shadows gathered about him as he watched her, contemplating how he might best relish these final moments before her light was, at last, smothered.

His voice was quiet, needling when he spoke. "You make me curious."

Penelope Grace remained silent, armored against his baiting this time.

Denagon, though, was not dismayed or discouraged by her lack of response. "Why is it that a plain, unexceptional girl such as yourself would come back so soon after her first failure?"

One deep breath and then, "I was called here."

He laughed, merciless, and mocking. "*Called?*" The shadows surrounding them deepened, creeping along the ground until the darkness closed around them, and, to the physical eye, Denagon and Penelope Grace were alone.

"Are you certain that you heard Him correctly?" Denagon continued. "Perhaps, you misunderstood. Could it be that your own pride called you here? Your own desperate need to be the hero?"

"No! He called me here, and here I will stay," she cried, a fire in her eyes whose source was altogether different from earthly flame.

Denagon paused, taking a step back. It struck him that he was not facing the same girl as he had in Svarthol, but of course, that mattered little to him. Denagon's smile was wicked as he closed in once more, confident that this girl would be just as easy to discourage.

"Very brave. But tell me, don't you ever wonder," and he said the word with a sneer, "how someone you believe to be so good would send someone like you to do something so impossible?"

The darkness rose, roiling in response to Denagon's hatred and pride until it seemed that all the world was only shadow and night.

Still, Penelope Grace stood her ground.

"What hope do you have? Do you really think it's possible to defeat me?" he asked, and this time, Penelope knew that the challenge demanded an answer.

"He forgave me for my pride."

Briefly, Denagon's eyes widened. "That old trick?"

"He sent a bold friend to expose my doubts for the lies that they are."

"You've tried this once before," he hissed, bearing down on her even as she spoke.

"I don't have the strength to defeat you," she confessed, and he stopped, unprepared for this.

Penelope Grace smiled. "But I know Someone Who does."

In an instant, a great, pure light began to shine, and the shadows around them dissipated. All around Penelope Grace, her friends and allies appeared, the peoples of Ellura fighting with remarkable bravery against the forces of darkness.

But just as a bold young fox had said, they were not alone.

Penelope Grace gasped as a winged being, entirely unlike the beasts they had fought, flew past her, overpowering one of Denagon's many slaves. Before she could quite make sense of what was happening, the sound of a great multitude of wings filled the air, overpowering even the countless shrieks rising from Denagon's army.

All around them, mighty angels fought, wielding brilliant blades as they fought against the many followers of darkness, while the sky itself seemed torn open with Light.

Penelope looked back down to find Denagon shrinking away, trembling, though not, Penelope realized, in fear of her. The Light grew ever more brilliant, and Denagon's eyes were fixed, even as they filled with hatred, on its Source.

Shaking herself, Penelope Grace turned around and could hardly breathe for the awe and wonder.

A figure approached, clothed in gleaming white. He looked like a man, but Penelope Grace was certain He was much more.

The world was ablaze at His coming, and she watched, captivated, as He accomplished what she could not.

"Keep away from me," Denagon hissed, seeming hardly able to form the words. Penelope looked at her enemy, only to find him fading in the face of the Light. He knelt, clawing at the earth as he looked up in fury at the One approaching as if hoping for some scrap of darkness to appear and provide refuge.

None could form in the Light's Presence, and he knew it, and he feared.

The figure was nearly upon him, and Denagon's form was now only palest grey against the white, snow-covered ground. He seemed to gasp for air, trying desperately to scramble away from the Light, and utterly powerless to do so.

At the last, he could only whisper bitterly, "I hate You. *I hate You.*"

But in the end, all the hatred in the world is only weakness in its most pitiable disguise, and the Light only shone more brilliantly, until all that surrounded them faded away in its radiance. Penelope was forced to shield her eyes.

The world fell silent, and it was some time before Penelope Grace opened her eyes to find Light restored, and an enemy, who had seemed so great, faded away to nothing at all.

An exultant bark reached her ears as her sight returned to normal. Penelope Grace looked around to find Tilly racing for her with a great burst of speed, her joy apparent and wonderfully contagious.

She looked around at the peoples and the land itself and saw rest given on every side. No sign remained of any of Denagon's creatures; each one had faded along with their defeated master.

Briefly, she looked around for some remnant of that brilliant Light, but neither He nor his angelic servants were visible either. Still, Penelope Grace was more aware of His steadfast presence than ever, and she began to understand that what could not be physically seen was not necessarily absent.

Tilly yipped once to regain her attention, then said, "Aye, lass, did I not tell ye that ye'd not be left alone?"

Warmth filled Penelope's face as she knelt down. "You are a bold friend, and I'm impossibly thankful that you were courageous enough to speak."

The fox looked down, uncharacteristically bashful at Penelope's words. "Well, someone had to set ye straight."

At that moment, Aira padded towards them, her eyes full of joy. Penelope wrapped her arms around Aira, burying her fingers in her warm, white fur. The wolf chuckled. "You did well, Penelope Grace."

She drew back. "Not on my own."

Together, the three picked their way through the battlefield, an altogether less joyous duty now in front of them. Though they had been given victory, many of Ellura's peoples had given their lives in the fight against Denagon.

Penelope's mood grew somber as, one by one, they gathered the bodies of their friends and prepared a final resting place for them all, worthy of their sacrifice. That night, once all the faithful fallen were laid to rest beneath the snow, the people of Ellura gathered as the evening sky grew bright with stars.

Aira and Elafry stood to either side of Penelope Grace as, one by one, the sprites and fairies alike rose up to the treetops, adding their blue and warm golden glow to the light of the stars. The forest beneath glimmered with the smattering of light, and Penelope wept for the impossible beauty of Light restored and for all those who were not here to see it.

Elafry pressed close to her. "Take courage, Penelope Grace. They are looking out now on a far better country."

Leaning on Elafry's shoulder, Penelope Grace closed her eyes, taking refuge once more in the hope of things to come.

She woke thinking of her family and longing to be reunited with them. But just as the thought crossed her mind, Penelope Grace was greeted by what sounded like music, and she knew frost fairies were hovering above her before she ever opened her eyes. She smiled, reminded of her very first morning in Ellura.

Sitting up, Penelope found the same group of frost fairies that had been sent for her in the underground stronghold, and yes, just there was the lavender-winged fairy who had made certain she was the one to deliver Arabella's message.

Penelope watched, bemused, as the same fairy once again pushed her way to the front of the group only to be met by an equally stubborn fairy with soft blue wings, who stared at her with an indignant look and an arched brow.

The lavender frost fairy rolled her eyes and offered a dramatic bow as she flew to the side, making way for her companion. Paying no mind to her antics, the second fairy flew forward with great dignity and spoke to Penelope. "The Ice Maiden requests that you meet with her, my lady."

"Of course," Penelope answered, fighting a laugh.

The group flew away, and Penelope Grace felt a bittersweet twinge as she watched them, wondering if ever she might see them again. But there was no more time to think of such things. Arabella waited for her, and then it would be time to return to her family.

She rose from the bed slowly, unsurprised by how her body ached all over, but soon enough, she was dressed and making her way toward Arabella's tent.

Upon entering, Arabella rose, clasping Penelope's hands in her own. "Penelope Grace, for all you have given and all you have surrendered, I thank you on behalf of all Ellura." As she spoke, the jewels in her necklace glimmered vibrantly, and Penelope remembered that the memories of this time in Ellura's history would be safeguarded there for the next Ismey.

"You don't need to thank me, Arabella. Had I not come to Ellura, both my family and I would be lost."

"Yes, your family. It is time you return to them. But first," the Ismey said with a smile, "I promised you a story."

Penelope Grace's breath caught in her throat; she had forgotten Arabella's promise to share the story of her grandmother's time in this place. She had waited so long to learn how the locket had come into her grandmother, Mary's, possession, and it was with great eagerness that she sat down to listen.

Much like her, dear reader, I imagine that your heart would both pound and break as you listened to the story of a broken melody and a heartsick girl.

But that story must wait for another winter.

Penelope Grace stood on a hill not far from the camp, which was now being slowly packed up, Aira at her side. Goodbyes had been shared with all of her friends, save the wolf, whom Penelope had asked to guide her back through the still unfamiliar land.

But she wanted a few moments more to soak in this impossibly real place.

Penelope Grace took in the frozen, snow-covered landscape, and she saw wonder, and she saw beauty, and she saw the anticipation of good things to come.

On the surface, winter may seem all death and drudgery, but look closely now, reader, and you'll see that winter is the springtime of the soul.

"Isn't it a wonder to see Light restored?" Aira asked softly.

"That it is, Aira. That it is."

Penelope met the wolf's gaze and, finding her own joy and sadness reflected there, could not bring herself to speak the words.

Aira spoke for her. "Time to go."

And she trotted down the hill, trusting that the young woman would follow.

Once more, Penelope Grace looked around at the land, set ablaze with warmth by all the sunlight and the snow, and thought of the many friends whom she loved with a lasting love. But she knew that the call now led away from them, and so, she ran, returning to a winter carousel and a quiet melody that would bring her home.

The music faded along with the swirling snow, and Penelope Grace stood once more in the forested park. Aira stood at the foot of the carousel's steps, waiting. She would remain with Penelope until she was safely returned home, an unspoken agreement between the two friends.

They began the journey through the park, and Penelope felt her pace quickening, so eager was she to return to her family now that she was so close to them. It seemed no time at all before they reached the end of her street, and Penelope slowed abruptly, wanting to savor these last remaining moments with her friend.

Still, it was only a few minutes more before the pair reached the steps leading up to her front door. Unable to think of truer words, Penelope Grace knelt to wrap her arms around her friend one last time and said, "I will miss you, Aira."

"Oh, Penelope Grace," the wolf tenderly replied, "if ever there is a need, you will be made able to find your way back to us." Aira pulled back to meet the young woman's gaze. "But if not, having known you at all is treasure enough."

Penelope smiled through gathering tears and forced herself to stand.

"Goodbye, dear friend," Aira said and turned to run down a cobblestone street through the softly falling snow.

Hesitantly, she turned the doorknob, wondering what she might find inside. But when she entered, the foyer was just as she remembered, welcoming, if not yet warm. Inside now, Penelope's nerves vanished, and she ran to the living room.

A few remaining tendrils of ice were vanishing even as she entered, but her parents and Nurse Sasha were where she had left them on that long-ago night. They remained frozen, but Penelope Grace was undeterred.

She rushed to her father, kneeling down before him and placing a warm hand upon his. Holding her breath in anticipation, Penelope watched as the ice began to disappear.

Quickly now, it faded away, replaced by the sudden warmth that flooded her father's frame. With a deep breath, he came awake and opened his eyes. Immediately, his gaze came to rest on Penelope, and his face lit up with joy and pride as he looked upon his daughter.

"My darling girl," John whispered, placing a loving hand upon her cheek.

"Papa," she cried, flinging her arms about him, impossibly overjoyed to see him smiling once again.

As she did, Georgie came rushing down the stairs with a cry of delight, while both her mother and Nurse Sasha woke to find a home once more filled with warmth and wonder and light. Penelope pulled back to take the sight of them all in, but she held still to her father's hands, unwilling yet to let them go.

Never could she have anticipated the simple gift of holding his hand in her own.

As the rest of their family gathered around them, Penelope Grace and John sat looking at each other, words insufficient to explain what they both knew: on the hardest of days, when wonder was most difficult to feel, and all light felt dim, they would be there to help the other see.

So concludes the adventures of
Penelope Grace and the Winter Carousel

AUTHOR'S GRATITUDE

If you asked me if I had any plans of writing *Penelope Grace and the Winter Carousel*, I would have to tell you, "No."

But I never could have anticipated my family's need for this story or my own.

Four years ago, on the darkest December day I will ever know, my grandpa, John, passed away. All through the following year, there was an emptiness and an ache that would not go away.

Something was missing.

Something wasn't right.

And I couldn't have told you what it was.

Until, on a cold night, God broke through the darkness that was suffocating our hearts and home. I opened up an old music box that my grandmother gave me when I was a little girl, and when I heard its melody, I saw a winter carousel turning and was introduced to the world of Ellura for the very first time.

I knew from the beginning that this would be a story about my mom, Penelope, and my grandpa, John. My mom is, without doubt, the most courageous woman of wonder I will ever know. But in the aftermath of losing her father, I saw wonder waning and wasn't content to watch it fade.

Every time I put pen to paper, I felt Light breaking through the darkness of grief and wonder sweeping away despair. I felt how relentlessly God was fighting for us in the midst of our pain, and I realized how kind He was to wait to give me this story until that particular time.

Never before had I considered wonder essential, never had I thought of it as a gift, let alone a weapon.

But it's all those things.

Wonder embodies the child-like faith that refuses to cower before circumstance.

Wonder is a gift from a loving, intentional Father Who knows that, without living in wonder of Him, the winters of our souls become hopelessly barren where they would otherwise be ablaze with preparation and hope.

Wonder is a sword that cuts through the lies that tell us faith is pointless, childish, and weak.

Wonder reminds us that our strength and our hope are rooted in Him.

When we were all left reeling from the loss of my grandpa, we needed a reminder of all these things.

And God, kind as He is, gave us that reminder in a story about a woman of wonder and a winter carousel, covered in snow.

I hope that, no matter what you might be facing or enduring right now, this story meets you there and reignites your sense of wonder in the One Who makes all things right and does all things well.

Now, for some gratitude to end this note:

To the One Who knew we needed wonder long before we did, Who restored it when we thought it was irretrievably lost. I will never be able to pen enough words to say thank You. I love You, too.

Penelope Grace (otherwise known as Mom): You are a wonder, and without your courageous example of loyalty and faith, I would never have had a reason to write this story. Are you looking forward to the next carousel ride as much as I am?

Dad: You are exactly the Dad I needed, and I'm so thankful that God was kind enough to let me be your daughter. I love you (even if you are a Codfish).

Big brother: Getting to be your little sis is one of the most remarkable blessings that God has, or ever will, give me. I am so proud of you, and I love you so much.

Grandpa: There are lessons I wish I had learned before I lost you. I love you with all my heart and will forever be missing you. Being your granddaughter was the great honor of my life.

Heather Pruitt, my fellow writer and friend: This writing journey can feel very lonely sometimes. Thank you so much for making it less so. (Go grab a copy of her wonderful story, *Anelthalien!* You'll love every moment of the adventure)

Erica, thank you so much for designing the most beautiful cover I could have hoped for and for being such a kind and faithful friend.

Callie, thank you so much for being the kindest, most steadfast friend during one of the hardest times of my life. I'm so grateful for you.

To my husband: God brought us together at a time when I was despairing of ever finding someone like you. What a wonder to find that the answer to every single one of my prayers was, "Yes." I love you, my heart.

To anyone who reads this story: God made wonder feel possible for us again, and I am so expectant for the way He is going to do the very same for you. Don't give up. The restoration of wonder is always worth the wait. Thank you so much for reading *Penelope Grace and the Winter Carousel*. Sharing this story with others is what makes the writing journey worthwhile.

If you enjoyed the story, please leave a review on Goodreads and Amazon — or any other review site — and share the tale with family and friends! You can join me on my writing adventures on www.2125Books.com and on social media, @2125Books

Alexandria Frederick
August 2025

ABOUT THE AUTHOR

Alexandria Frederick is a Christian fantasy author and owner of 21:25 Books, an independent publishing company. She loves stories that draw readers' hearts back to God and remind them that light is always overcoming darkness. Her first novel was *Penelope Grace and the Winter Carousel*. Alexandria lives in Ohio with her husband, daughter, and their menagerie of animals. She is currently off somewhere, writing about dragons and brewing a pot of coffee. You can join her writing adventures at www.2125Books.com

www.ingramcontent.com/pod-product-compliance
Lightning Source LLC
LaVergne TN
LVHW041641060526
838200LV00040B/1662